Mary Christmas

Hanna Park

Baisong Press

This is a work of fiction. Names, characters, places, and incidents are either the product of the author's imagination or are used fictitiously, and any resemblance to actual persons living or dead, business establishments, events, or locales is entirely coincidental.

Mary Christmas

Cover Art by *Niki White* www.nikiawhiteart.com

Visit Hanna Park at www.hannapark.ca

Baisong Press, PO Box 291, Port Carling, ON P0B 1J0

First Edition, 2024

Digital ISBN, 978-1-0689975-1-8

Paperback ISBN, 978-1-0689975-2-5

Published in Canada

Praise for Hanna Park

Hanna Park's Finding Tiegan skillfully weaves a tapestry of romance, mystery, and the intriguing concept of fate.

— Literary Titan

Park weaves this heart-wrenchingly beautiful story with steam and silliness—Unwrapped in Roros

— Paranormal Romance Guild

I'm a big fan of Hanna Park's books because she writes erotic romance with an artistic soul. You'll be swept up in the experience of falling in love while reading.

— N.N. Heaven

to those who believe

Chapter One

Mary

Festive tunes floated to every nook of Bell's Department Store, the one big box store in Forest Falls. Soaring high into the foyer, the magnificent Norway spruce twinkled with tiny white lights and glass baubles glimmering with silver and gold. The countdown was on.

"Merry Christmas, Mrs. Sandusky." I tilted my head, taking one last look at the rectangular box, its shiny paper corners neatly folded and adorned with a silver ribbon and bow. I handed the gift to the older woman. "I'm certain Mr. Sandusky will love his new sweater."

Wrapping presents—tearing sheets of shiny paper from the rack—just enough, but not too much, was fun. Too much sticky tape gluing my fingers together... The icy wind rolling through the revolving doors on the heels of every shopper and freezing my feet? Like I said—fun.

"Thank you so much, Mary. The way you wrap these presents is lovely. It's a shame to open them. Just lovely, dear. Just lovely." Mrs. Sandusky had lived in this town her entire life. The gentle soul swept her gray hair over her ear and smiled. "Will we be seeing you Saturday at the pancake social?"

"I wouldn't miss it for the world, Mrs. Sandusky." I lifted my eyebrows and grinned, appreciating her enthusiasm for the Christmas fundraiser in Memorial Park two days from now.

There were only two ways to arrive in Forest Falls: the winding road that meandered through the tree-covered valleys or the steam train. The tourists preferred the steam train's magical allure. Nestled on the 45th parallel, halfway to the North Pole, and surrounded by mountains, our little town offered a secluded haven for families and those seeking a quiet retreat. I was the oddity, the one who never married and never left.

The nights were long in Forest Falls.

"The Rotary Club's handing out turkeys. One hundred turkeys." She clapped her hands together. "Isn't that wonderful?"

"Amazing." I nodded and looked up, drawn to the booming "Ho. Ho. Ho." of the store Santa echoing down the center aisle. Nestled in a blanket of synthetic snow, Santa's Wonderland was open for business, the big elf welcoming a long lineup of merry faces.

"The town is so busy, dear. I'm not sure where all these people come from." She shook her head back and forth, looking at me for an answer.

"It's a good thing, Mrs. Sandusky." She referred to the holiday visitors converging on our little town.

Forest Falls, aka Christmastown—boutiques filled with woolens, galleries stuffed with paintings, and the quaint brick buildings lining the street. And then there was the snow—the abundance of white, fluffy flakes blanketing the town from November through March. Enter the magic.

Falling in love was inevitable.

My thoughts drifted to the Riverside, the neighborhood cafe—where I could be curled up in one of those overstuffed wing chairs, warming my toes by the crackling fireplace and indulging in a steaming latte.

I set my gaze on the strands of ribbon cluttering my workbench while Tinsel, my blue merle collie cross, snored softly in her candy-striped bed. The silver ruff around her neck earned the name Tinsel from the local rescue.

"Mary? Mary Christmas? Is that you?" The deep timber of a voice from Christmas past reverberated through my bones like the wind sighing through the trees.

I looked up and into a lake-blue gaze rife with mischief.

Christopher Northbrook—tall and striking, with well-defined masculine features, flashed a dazzling smile, ripping my heart into two distinct pieces.

My boyfriend, in another life.

The soft skin around his eyes crinkled, revealing a once familiar expression—the boy who made me crazy in all the right ways. Everyone loved Christopher. When he wasn't erupting into laughter, he was making someone smile.

As my mother liked to say, the one who got away.

"Mary, how are you?" He swept his fingers through a tousled head of hair, the color of the night sky, gazing at me beneath dark eyebrows.

I took a slow, deep breath and stared at his black turtleneck, the fine merino wool defining his muscular form. Dumbstruck would be the correct word to describe my reaction.

"Christopher?" I dug my fingernails into my palms, stemming the heat flowing to my face.

He dropped four toys on the table: a firetruck, a dump truck, and two giant dinosaurs. He looked into my eyes and said, "For my kids."

"Kids?" I delved through ten years of muddled memories. No one had ever mentioned Christopher having kids—married, yes, but kids?

"And you've got a dog? Since when do you like dogs?" His lush mouth quirked upward. He slipped his hands into the pockets of his khaki-green parka, his manner more casual than nonchalant.

"I love dogs, Christopher. I volunteer at the shelter every weekend." I sat my hands on my hips, realizing too late that I had fallen for his teasing banter.

"It's been a long time, Mary Christmas. Look at you, as beautiful as ever. How the world has changed, though." His voice, a deep, sensual caress.

Oh yeah, I had a history with this man. Christopher graduated high school with a full scholarship to an Ivy League school and returned fresh out of university. Six months later, he proposed, and in all my Mary wisdom, I had turned him down.

His return baffled me. His parents had left the far north for sunnier climes, and he and his sister had never been close. I shot him a sidelong glance.

"Six-year-old twins. Alfie and Dash." He pulled his phone from his pocket, displaying his phone's screen—two little boys, identical in every way to their father, smiled back.

"Twins?" I gazed at the photo.

Ten years ago, I buried a heart-wrenching love and spent every day since hiding from the loss. I hugged my arms across my chest, confused by his friendly demeanor.

"It's been a while, yeah?" He slid his phone back into his pocket.

"I didn't know you had children. Congratulations, Christopher." A rock settled in the pit of my stomach. I leaned forward, fighting a wave of dizziness.

"It's just me and the boys now...Isabelle passed away four years ago." The shadows flickering across his face gave me pause.

"I'm sorry to hear that." A shiver passed through me, along with a sense of loss—my grandfather and my father lost within the same year. I looked at him in a new light. Raising two young boys alone could not be easy.

"Time passes." The twinkle in his eyes wavered, although his gaze remained fixed on me.

"I heard you got into the brokerage business. Hedge funds?" I said too quickly.

"An opportunity presented itself—one I couldn't turn down." He inclined his head. "Hey, guess what? I bought the old Maguire place. We're going to be neighbors."

"What? You're moving back?" Seeing him sent a riot of emotions racing through me. I yearned to touch him—not that I would.

"I can't wait to get started." A dreamy expression crossed his face, his love for everything broken, and the Maguire place was just that: abandoned and left to the wilds of the wind.

But this, this was something else entirely. He did not know what forces were at play. The Maguires didn't leave their home willingly. But fear does that to people.

"We're staying with my sister until the house is livable." He pinched his chin between his thumb and index finger, his gaze never straying.

Tinsel whimpered, making her presence known.

"Would you like name cards?" I grinned like a loon.

They say time flies when you're having fun.

"Please... These are for Alfie, and these are for Dash." He separated the gifts, his smile widening.

My gaze lowered to the expensive watch strapped around his strong wrist, to the hands that once held me tight. I pushed the red pom-pom dangling in my face behind my ear.

"How are you, Mary? Do you have kids? Who's the lucky guy who captured Mary's heart?" He waited for my answer.

"Excuse me?" I brushed my hands over my stretchy green tights, considering how I must look. An ugly Christmas sweater? A green felt hat? Festive? Yes. Glamorous? Not.

"Chelsea told me you were getting married. I was glad for you, Mary." He held my gaze.

Chelsea...I pictured his sister, blonde and blue-eyed. We graduated from Forest High in the same year. I was the prom queen, and she was the drama queen. She never forgave me for winning that title. Why would she say I was married? I told myself it didn't matter. He moved on. I hadn't.

"No, I never married." I glared at my feet, engulfed in pointed elf shoes. No one else had turned my world upside down, and no one else had compared.

"But I thought. Oh...my mistake." His brows furrowed.

"Any wrapping in mind?" I gestured toward the rolls of wrapping paper suspended on the rack. Candy canes, stripes, and reflective foil—the possibilities were endless.

"You be the judge, Mary Christmas." He turned his wrist, checking his watch.

"They'll be ready in ten." I gulped, swallowing the

lump in my throat—longing and sadness mixed into one big, bouncy ball.

"Sounds good." His gaze lingered too long, far too long.

"Okay." I fidgeted, twisting my fingers into the hem of my sweater—the threads unraveling. I lost sight of him in a sea of bobbing heads, envisioning his smiling face with every crinkle of paper and every twirling ribbon.

I tied name tags onto each wrapped gift and set them aside. I could avoid him. I didn't have to see him—much. It wasn't entirely impossible. After all, I spent most of my time on Christmas Mountain. A tide of emotion swept through me, and I didn't know what to do with it.

"Mary? Mary, are you all right?" Aredhel blended into the community as a full-time assistant at the nearby law office. Yet, every holiday season, she couldn't resist showing her true nature at Bell's Department Store as one of Santa's elves—for shits as giggles as she put it. She tapped her candy cane-painted fingernails on the tabletop, her singsong voice calling me from my musings.

"What? Oh. Yep, I'm good. What's up?" My gaze locked with hers, and I smiled, a sense of calm flowing over me—Aredhel, my longest friend. Still, the aura surrounding her always took me by surprise. She was otherworldly, with stunning violet eyes framed by flaxen tresses like corn silk worn loose over her pointed ears.

"There's a bunch of us going to the holiday flick. Wanna come?" She tilted her chin. The weekly routine amongst the staff was a night out at the Spinning Reel, the movie theater on the main street.

"Oh, I can't tonight. But thanks. Next week, for sure." I made excuses, savoring the idea of a hot bath and bed and Christopher. Not.

"What's going on with you? You look like you've seen a

ghost." She set her hand on my cheek, her shadowed eyes expressing deep concern.

The circular clock hanging over the entrance door ticked the minutes by, second by second. The lights dimmed, warning shoppers that the closing was near.

"Nothing, I'm fine." I busied myself with something, anything. I rearranged Christopher's presents, gazing down the empty aisle. What if he didn't return in time?

"Mach-a latte with oat milk. Right?" Christopher placed a takeaway cup from the Riverside Cafe onto the table, the cold scent of winter blending with his intoxicating scent.

I whipped my head his way and loosed a sigh. My tongue darted across my parched lips.

Aredhel's gaze swept back and forth. Her smile turned devious. "Well, I'll leave you to it, babe. Maybe we'll see you at the movies." She gave me a thumbs-up and skipped down the aisle, her elf shoes jingling.

"Oh, geez. Thanks, you didn't need to do that." That familiar longing gripped my heart.

"Hey, it's the least I can do. You didn't tell me who this is?" He circled my table and dropped onto his heels, extending his palm toward Tinsel. "Well, hello there, pretty girl."

"This is Tinsel. She's a rescue." My eyes widened when Tinsel hurtled into his arms, wiggling her butt a million miles an hour—the traitor.

"She's beautiful." He stroked Tinsel's head. "This is what I want—a big old house the boys can get lost in with a dog sleeping in front of a blazing fire." His smile grew as he rose to his full height, brushing silver strands from his dark jeans. "It was great seeing you, Mary. I hope we can get together sometime. It would be nice to catch up." His voice, the soft purr of a lover's caress.

Did I imagine the look of longing passing through his eyes?

As the distance between us lengthened, I called after him, "Goodbye, Christopher, and welcome home."

* * *

The clock struck nine, and the last shopper left the store. I dallied in the staff room, removing my elf shoes and pulling on my snowpacks. I shrugged into my puffer coat and pulled on my toque. Tinsel whined. I crossed my arms and sighed. I considered Aredhel's invitation. Driving home in a snowstorm and spending another night alone had somehow lost its charm.

"Good night, Mary." Bob, the security guard, unlocked the staff door into the back parking lot.

"Night, Bob." I walked down the few steps, Tinsel beside me.

A stiff wind howled mercilessly, swaying the trees and taking my breath along with it. I balled my hands into fists, calling the fury and calming the storm. I breathed out a warm breath, which froze into icy particles.

When my grandfather passed, he left me Christmas's Christmas Tree Farm, ten thousand acres of forested hills and valleys, and his trust that I would carry on the family legacy. Like my grandfather and his father before him, I safe-guarded our ancestors' secrets. With the last name of Christmas, magic ran in our blood, and along with that, a secret I'd diligently kept for so many years, even from Christopher.

I stuffed my hands into my pockets, stared at my car, at

the broken wiper blade, and chastised myself for not completing the repair while the sun shone.

"Let's go for a walk, Tinsel." I snapped the lead onto her collar, heading toward the downtown bustle and hum. I sighed happily, gazing down the main street toward the train station. From the two-story red brick buildings and the cobblestone sidewalks to the lampposts casting a golden gaslight onto the streets below, Forest Falls held those who visited in a magical grip.

I loved this place.

The snow began to fall as I weaved through the crowds, strolling along the main street. Along the broad avenue, trees glittered with iridescent lights.

For the first time in a long time, I felt alive.

The train's whistle, a high-pitched blast, turned every head. I took note of the town clock, glowing like a beacon—right on time. The train chugged through town on its departing journey. On a clear night, pungent fingers of soot floated on the gentle breezes that were always afoot.

The latest arrivals spoke excitedly and pointed toward the frozen banks of the Pretty River, where the cobbled path sparkled with a rainbow of flickering lights, and the skating trail was lit with fiery torches. They bounced their rolling suitcases over the icy ruts, making their way toward the shining lights of Forest Falls' only hotel, The Pretty River Inn, overlooking the falls.

Mrs. Sandusky was right about the influx of people, but the tourists flocking to our town brought money they were happy to spend—something the retailers desperately needed.

"Get a grip, Mary. Your life is fine—it's more than fine. It's good. It's great." I gazed upward into the falling snow, allowing the wet flakes to cool my heated cheeks. Words—

only words—my soul said something else. Seeing Christopher, if only for a moment, dredged up so many unrequited feelings. I tried to bury them.

Tinsel's adoring eyes met mine, and she wagged her tail.

I lingered in front of Bell's Christmas windows, an enchanting display of elves draped in green tunics pounding hammers on wooden blocks. Wrapped in a ruby-red dress and cinched with a flowing green bow, one elf placed a silver bauble on a shimmering tree.

"Merry Christmas, Mary," Sam tilted his flat cap and smiled.

"Hello, Sam. How's Matilda?" I glanced at the town's pharmacist, now the proud owner of the local apothecary, locking the door to his shop.

"Expecting any day now. I'm keeping my fingers crossed for a Christmas delivery." He placed his hands on his plump belly and chuckled.

"Give her a big hug from me." My heart burst with joy for the growing family. I considered them good friends.

I covered my eyes, blinded by the beaming headlights of one car after another. Topped with snow, they resembled fluffy marshmallows, their rolling tires crunching the packed snow.

Tinsel whined, pulling me toward the carousel in the middle of the park. Blinking with festive red lights, steam whistled through the calliope, whimsically and slightly off-key. Intricate cutouts crowned the canvas roof, and a red flag fluttered in the breeze.

The nostalgic circus tune made my heart sing.

The golden chariots stayed on the circular platform while the horses swept outward, causing the little ones to hang on for dear life as they galloped through the air. I zeroed in on two little boys flying by on two magnificent steeds. The boys, dressed in neon orange snowsuits and matching green toques, waved their red-mitten hands at their dad.

From my vantage point, I witnessed what should have been a heartwarming scene.

Christopher stood on the cobblestone path, towering over his sister. I caught the odd word and realized they were talking about me. My first impulse was to turn and walk away.

Chelsea spotted me first, her scowl turning into a wide smile.

"Well, if it isn't Mary Christmas. How are you, sweetie? Are you still at the bakery?" She tucked her coiffed blonde hair behind her ear, her diamond earrings catching the moonlight.

"Merry Christmas, Chelsea. Yes, my mother still owns the bakery. I help when I can." She traveled in different circles than I did. Married to Lincoln Frost, the mayor of Forest Falls, they lived in 'Snob Hill,' a beautiful enclave of estate homes overlooking the river.

"I would never abandon Lincoln for such trivial pursuits, but then again, it takes all kinds." She hooked her hand around Christopher's elbow.

"Chelsea." His voice bristled. He shot an apologetic glance my way.

Tinsel recognized Christopher and sprinted forward. Chelsea stepped sideways, her smile fading.

"You're living at the farm, I suppose?" She looked down her nose, her thin lips attempting a smile.

"Yes, that's correct." I chuckled, unable to recall the last time Chelsea Northbrook had been nice to me. I resisted the urge to start a snowball fight.

"Dad. Dad." Two soprano voices rang out, "Can we do

it again? Can we, Dad?" They stopped short when they saw Tinsel, their blue eyes beaming.

Tinsel lumbered toward the boys, almost identical in size, and sat down in the snow.

"Can we pat your dog?" Alfie looked at me, his gaze hopeful.

"Yes, you can. That's very smart of you to ask." I shot a quick glance at Christopher, who was looking on.

"What's her name?" Dash sat on his heels and offered his hand toward Tinsel.

"Her name is Tinsel, and she's friendly." I placed my hand on her ruff, encouraging her.

"Boys, this is my friend, Mary." His lips peeled into a smile. He stepped forward and rested his hand on my elbow.

My heartbeat thundered as I stared at the boys, who looked so much like their father. Their dark, curly hair peeked under their hats, and their lake-blue eyes were curious.

"These are my boys, Alfie and Dash." He looked from one to the other, his voice filled with pride.

"Dad, can we get a dog?" Alfie crowded Tinsel, his little face smiling from ear to ear.

"Hey, have you boys written your letters to Santa Claus yet?" I pointed to the red mailbox at the walkway's edge, marking Santa's Express in swirling letters. "Your dad can help you. There's still time."

They looked at me with serious faces and wonder dancing in their eyes. My chest tightened.

"Christopher, we need to leave." She tugged her brother's sleeve. "I left the oven on."

I watched her watching me.

"It was nice seeing you again, Mary." He searched my face and then turned to leave. "Boys, let's go."

"It was nice meeting you, Alfie. You too, Dash." I stood in the snow and watched the boys jumping up and down, with their dad clasping each orange snowsuit with one hand.

Whatever our past relationship, it was just that—in the past. I tugged gently on Tinsel's lead, returning her to my side. The need to fill my mind with anything else over-whelmed my thoughts.

The line moved quickly beneath the triangular marquee jutting out over the sidewalk, hundreds of white lightbulbs flickering in random sequence. I took a moment to admire the glowing movie posters adorning the brick facade. Once a venue for vaudeville performances, the historic theater preserved its century-old allure with its eye-catching art deco decor. I rifled through my wallet for the entrance fee.

"Hi, Mary. I wondered if we'd see you tonight." Trent stood behind the glassed-in ticket booth, jutting onto the sidewalk. He handed me a ticket stub. "The gang's all here."

"I almost didn't, but here I am." I smiled, walking through the glass doors, greeted by the intoxicating aroma of hot buttered popcorn.

"Mary! There you are," Aredhel, who looked spectac-ular as usual, wore a cherry red halterneck mesh playsuit, the ruched front floating to her upper thighs. Eye-catching, to say the least. Her arms were loaded with three extra-large buckets of golden popcorn and a cardboard tray filled with three cream sodas.

I smiled. Aredhel knew me too well.

"JoJo saved our seats, front row center." She strode through the swinging doors, giving the well-dressed usher an appraising glance.

He reacted as most men did in Aredhel's presence—staring longingly in her direction.

"Let me help you." I relieved Aredhel of the three popcorn buckets and stepped down a sloping aisle flanked by rows of plush seats and crimson-draped walls.

"Hey, you made it." Jojo jumped from her chair, relieving me of the soda pop.

"You look nice." I smiled, admiring the form-fitting and fringed sweater dress landing mid-thigh. "I love the color," I commented on the rich chocolate shade.

"Thanks, Miranda's is having a sale. You have to go." She slurped soda through her straw. "Oh, and look at these boots. I found them at Here and There." She twisted sideways, showing off knee-high winter-white leather boots.

"Spill the tea, girl. Who was the hottie?" Aredhel's melodic voice rang out as the lights blinked and dimmed, the feature film flashing across the silver screen. She hadn't been in town long enough to know the man who held my heart.

"A hottie? What hottie?" JoJo tossed popcorn into her mouth, her brown eyes wide behind her thick plastic frames. JoJo knew. Oh yeah, she knew the whole sordid tale.

"Christopher." I took a deep breath and closed my eyes against the flashing screen and the blaring soundtrack. "Christopher's back."

My voice cracked. His name. His face. Everything about him played havoc with my shattered heart.

Chapter Two

Christopher

The world sat beneath the shroud of twilight, dawn breaking the horizon. Laden with sleep, my thoughts drifted into the borderland, then snapped to attention. I lurched into a sitting position, surveying the dark space, which was unfamiliar and unsettling. Staying at my sister's and her husband's house didn't sit well with me. We were a welcome imposition.

I swung my legs to the carpeted floor, my eyes adjusting to the dim light.

I donned light-weight running pants, slipped into a long-sleeved base layer, and, with quiet stealth, descended the winding staircase, each tread creaking softly beneath my feet.

I left Forest Falls believing nothing was left for me, and I never looked back. The last ten years were a whirlwind, brimming with happiness yet fraught with sadness.

I tiptoed through the foyer in sock feet, stepped into my running shoes, closing the door softly behind me.

My breath clouded, icy particles hanging in the frosty air. Powdered with snow, the trees sat silent, slumbering through the wintry chill. I cocked my head and listened to the birdsong welcoming the dawn, the muffled hoot of an owl in a nearby tree, and perhaps the huff of an angry raccoon.

I zipped up my windbreaker and searched my pockets for the waterproof gloves I had stashed there.

I hit the pavement and followed the road with a long stride, passing by expansive lawns and identical two-story homes—dark silhouettes stark against the gray skies.

Crossing paths with Mary was a revelation. She was the girl of my dreams. I had forgotten how beautiful she was— her strawberry hair streaked with gold and emerald eyes fringed with long lashes. Seeing her again, with her lips quirking into that slight smile, sent a wave crashing over me, thawing the ice in my veins.

When I learned she had never married, the frozen glacier within me fractured into a million shards. Shock-waves thundered through my being as those icy fragments pierced my defenses, freeing me from a prison I had created for myself—four years of solitary confinement. I lived like a monk with no room for another.

I turned, detecting the thundering roar of the nearby waterfalls, and relived the moment we met. I slowed my pace, the ground icy underfoot.

We had moved to Forest Falls in my twelfth summer. While Chelsea spent every moment at the movie theater, I explored the mighty forest surrounding our home. Forest Falls began as a mining town deep in the Canadian north at the base of two intersecting mountains, and when the mines shut down, the town was forgotten—but the mines, those intersecting crevices, and caverns held great appeal. I had done my research, and with an old mining map and the river as my guide, I set out to Christmas Mountain.

The river trickled down the mountainside, cutting through rugged granite formations and cascading over tumbled rocks. A song played in the breeze, and my ears pricked up. I followed the whispering notes until I was completely disoriented. A green canopy stretched as far as I could see, and the forest floor glimmered with diamond light—a stone-grey face rose into the clouds. Rounding the trunk of a giant tree, I spotted a red-haired nymph high up in the branches, whistling the sweetest and most intricate notes. She pelted acorns at me and sent me running, only solidifying my made-up mind. Girls were to be avoided at all costs.

Our second encounter changed my mind—with the wind flying through my hair and my feet stuck out to the sides, riding my bicycle. That's where she found me. Scarred and bloody, sprawled face-first on the dirt road bordering the old Maguire place, abandoned even then. She dragged me back to Christmas's Christmas Tree Farm, where her mother tended to my wounds. We had shared popsicles, and she had introduced me to her pet goat, Fa La La La La.

Getting lost in the woods with Mary was once the highlight of my life. Agile and sure-footed, she could blend into the shadows, appearing out of nowhere, her laughter rippling in the quiet wood.

With Mary, I could breathe.

I ventured down tree-lined streets into the old part of town.

After Isabelle, running became a passion, the one thing that kept me sane. The boys had little memory of their mother. To them, she was a smiling face in a picture frame.

Leaving the city was an easy decision. Raising two active boys in a high-rise condo in a big downtown city no longer made sense. I woke one morning to sirens blaring, resolute in my decision, and I left my career behind, a happier man for it.

Last night, I tossed and turned. My mind followed my heart into the netherworld, where desire took shape and form, and into an enchanting realm where dreams and wishes come true. I woke tangled in bedsheets, her name whispered on my lips.

She was mine, and I was hers—until the day she refused me. The truth lay buried in the backyard of my mind.

She never married.

I let that realization sink in.

"Why did you tell me Mary was getting married?" I asked *my sister, confusion clawing at my thoughts.*

"What?" Chelsea's expression remained unchanged.

"When I met Isabelle. When you came to the city." The mirror cracked, revealing the truth.

"Christopher?" She pursed her painted lips into a tight line. "That woman was never good enough for you."

"So you lied to me." I closed my eyes for a brief second, realizing the truth.

"I gave you a push in the right direction. What's wrong with that?" She lifted her eyebrows and looked away.

And then Mary appeared, bathed in the moon's glow, with snowflakes dancing in the sky. It was almost magical. Chelsea attempted to embarrass her, but Mary deftly blocked the emotional attack. Her radiance only intensified.

I slowed as I approached the train station, struck by its stunning craftsmanship—its flowing shape and proportions: the intricate roof design, the extended porte-cochères, and the jutting telegrapher's bay. I stopped to appreciate the artistry of the exposed rafter tails, the entrance pillars, and the uniquely shaped shingles.

The conductor stood beneath the closest overhang, sharing a cup of coffee with the ticket master. When I left, they both waved.

From there, I ran the center line, empty of vehicular traffic at this time of day. Six blocks of commercial activity—not much had changed in the past ten years. There was a constant about the place, a steadying force. Maybe it was the surrounding wilderness, untouched for so many years. Or the mist that hung in the valley. It made me wonder.

The main street slept except for one shop: Something Sweet, a bakery owned and operated by Mary's mother. Even at this hour, light shone through a star-shaped window in the kitchen door, emitting a sparkling beam through the store and onto the snow-covered street. I peered through the glass and saw bare counters and empty displays.

I tapped on the door once, twice, and then a third time.

Mary appeared as I knew she would, her hair wrapped in a pink headband. She stuck her head through the kitchen door, looked about the store, and stared at the dark window.

Basked in the glow of the kitchen light, she looked like an angel.

"We're closed." She rubbed her temples, leaving a dusting of white flour behind.

Her voice reminded me of tinkling bells.

"Mary, it's me. Christopher." I pressed my hands against my face, my breath fogging the glass.

Recognition dawned on her face, indecision floating through her emerald eyes. She walked to the door, her slender figure concealed beneath a white chef's coat and a pink polka-dot apron.

"What are you doing here?" She unlatched the door and peeked out the narrow gap.

"Morning run. Why are you here?" I placed my hand on the door jamb and broke into a cold sweat. She could send me on my way here and now, dashing my every hope.

"I work here." She nibbled the corner of her mouth.

"Are you going to let me in?" My chest tightened as I watched her.

"I'm busy, Christopher." She tossed her hand, motioning toward the empty shelves.

"Do you need a hand? Throw me an apron. I'd be happy to help." I flashed her my best smile.

"You're serious?" She smiled back, her eyes shimmering like fire.

"I'm always serious. I'm a serious guy." I removed my gloves and shoved them into my pocket. A silent moment passed between us.

"Well, that's not the Christopher I remember." She looked unconvinced.

"Things changed. I changed." I offered my open palms in a gesture of goodwill. "Are you always working the morning shift?" I reached out and tugged the tie of her pink apron.

"Stop it." She swatted my hand and huffed. "I'm making sticky buns, okay? For the Mayor's Address."

"The Mayor's Address? What's that?" I brushed my hand through my hair, shaking snowflakes down the back of my windbreaker.

"Yes, the Mayor's Holiday Message. It's a big deal. The whole town attends—the Pancake Festival and Free Turkey Day. Surely your sister told you? The town admin hired Something Sweet to provide the desserts, and Riverwalk is making the hot chocolate." She folded her arms over her chest.

"Not a bad gig." My heart twisted in my chest. I had never forgotten the look of confusion on her face when I turned and walked away. I had missed something—something important. I could see that now. Then, disappointment blinded me.

"I guess." She pursed her lips into a bow and then scrunched her nose.

"Let me in. I can help." I shifted sideways, pushed forward by a gust of wind. Whispers teased my mind.

"Fine. Lock the door behind you." She swung the door wide and walked away from me.

I followed her through the swinging door and into the back kitchen, inhaling the sweet, sugary notes. I gazed at the sparkling stainless-steel counters and commercial ovens lining the wall.

"Wow. I'm blown away. Did you make these?" I looked from one rack to another, stacked with waving gingerbread men.

"Do you know how to decorate cookies?" She planted her hand on the curve of her hip.

"I thought you said sticky buns?" I removed my jacket and hung it on the back door.

She motioned toward the double ovens loaded with sheets of miniature muffin tins.

"That's a lot of sticky buns. Is that your grandfather's recipe?" I peered through the glass door at the rising puffs, swirled with a buttery brown sugar and cinnamon concoction.

"Yes. That's why I'm in charge of sticky buns." She sniffed.

"Where is your mother?" I searched the kitchen corners, half expecting the lady to appear.

"Hawaii."

"Hawaii?"

"She goes away every year." She buzzed from one counter to the other, preparing this and that.

"Since when?" I leaned back, an unexpected happiness settling into my soul.

"Since Howard. Her latest love. They travel every-where." She pointed toward a wall calendar. "Cruising the Antarctica in January, Fiji in February."

"And you're what? Running this place? Working at Bells? And who's managing the farm?" I scratched my forehead.

"Me. Well, it's not all me. I have help—good help. I couldn't run either place otherwise." She enchanted me with her smile.

The oven alarm beeped, drawing her attention from me. She turned, swung the double doors open, and then jumped back in a cloud of hot steam.

"That's not what I meant." I let out a sharp breath.

"What?" She looked up from the multiple trays, her brows pinched together.

"You're alone at Christmas?" I lifted my chin, consid-ering the facts. She lived alone, a long way from town.

"Oh, I guess. Not really. I have Tinsel and, you know, the farm. I have a lot to look after. I can't leave." She said in a quiet voice.

Bells rang in my mind, taking me back so many years ago. That's what she had said—I can't leave.

"What can I do? Show me." I grabbed a hair net and stuffed the fine mesh over my head.

"You mean it? You want to help?" She pinned her lips together, hiding her laughter.

"Yes." I nodded. "Where do you want me?"

"Okay." She tossed a polka-dot apron identical to hers my way and smirked.

"Okay." I pulled the neck loop over my head and tied it back.

"Very chic." She handed me a piping bag filled with white icing.

I held the plastic cone in both hands, questioning my abilities, my confidence failing.

"Watch." She expertly outlined the first gingerbread man, moving from one to another with the skill of a matador in a bull ring.

"Okay, let me try." I began with a big blob of white, which overflowed onto the parchment paper, my hands two clumsy bear paws.

"That's fine. Try again." She added a zigzag here and a ripple there, then switched to red and green icing, creating perfect buttons and pretty bows. "Do the faces. Two eyes and a smile."

"Like this?" I dabbed, dabbed, and zipped.

"Perfect, I think you've got it." Her eyes twinkled, her voice full of light.

"I want to apologize for yesterday." I looked up and then down. One, two, three, four. I managed five happy faces. I turned, facing her.

"What are you talking about?" She brushed her forehead with the back of her hand, pinned her bottom lip beneath her teeth, and continued decorating.

"Chelsea—her behavior was uncalled for." I rested my chin on my thumb, recalling Chelsea's hurtful words.

"Oh." She dipped the one sticky bun into a ceramic bowl, dousing it with a frosty glaze, and set it aside.

"I'm sorry, Mary. She can be difficult." I studied her, confused by her calm demeanor. I had seen Chelsea fly into a rage—my sister didn't know the meaning of calm.

"It's fine. It's just Chelsea." She placed a white cardboard box tied with a string on the counter. "Take these for the boys. A dozen gingerbread cookies."

"You don't need to do that." I turned to her, touched by her kindness.

"I want to." Her smile reached her eyes.

I leaned in, brushing flour from the tip of her nose. Was it even possible to rekindle the love we once had?

"Christopher." She lowered her chin and stared right through me.

"I want what we once had—I want it back." I cupped her elbow, gazing into limpid pools.

The entrance door rattled, bringing the here and now into Something Sweet's kitchen. It rattled again and then stopped.

"Can I see you again?" The thought of not touching her was almost painful.

"No. No, we can't. I can't." She turned her face from me.

"Mary, look at me..." I traced the underside of her jaw with my fingertips, her apple blossom scent washing over me.

"We can't just start up where we left off." She met my gaze, her eyes shimmering with sunset gold.

"You never stop loving someone you once loved," I whispered words straight from my heart.

"Wait." She spun on her heels and walked away. She returned, shoving the baker's box into my hands.

"I need to see you again." I resisted the urge to kiss her sweet lips.

"Have a nice day, Christopher." She touched my fingers, sending heated sparks flying. She drew in a sharp breath and looked away.

I knew then that the fire raging between us could not be quenched. Not now. Not ever.

I wanted to reach out and pull her into my arms. I needed her to look at me, to see me. I would convince her, if it took all my days, that I wasn't that boy any longer and that I would never hurt her again.

"Goodbye, Mary." I turned and walked away. The door closed behind me, filling the bakery with tinkling bells.

Wondrous star-shaped flakes fell from a cloudy sky. Two white-tailed deer stood on the river bank. An older man turned his head, watching me with curiosity. I couldn't wipe the smile from my face.

* * *

"What's that, Dad?" Alfie sat on the high bar stool, his knees tucked beneath him, leaning across the marble island in my sister's kitchen.

"Good morning. You're up early." Chelsea shot me a playful glance from the nearby pantry. Without makeup and with her hair tousled, she evoked memories of the cheerful girl she used to be rather than the polished adult preoccupied with keeping up appearances.

I untied the bow and opened the box, the fragrant aroma of perfectly decorated gingerbread cookies filling the room. The boys crowded the box, inhaling notes of molasses and ginger, cinnamon, and spice.

"Oh, can I have one?" Dash dived in.

"Of course." I leaned on my elbows, watching their eyes briefly close as they savored each bite. I reached for one myself.

"You went to the bakery? To her bakery?" Chelsea snapped her head toward me, accusation written all over her face.

"I did. These are freshly baked boys. Compliments to Mary. Do you remember Mary and Tinsel? And your good old dad even helped with the icing." My mind wandered back to the bakery, her laughter ringing in my mind.

"I remember Tinsel. Can we get a dog, Dad? Can we?" Dash pleaded, his mouth full of gingerbread cookies.

"One day, we will. Dash. I promise." I patted his head.

"Not in this house. I'm sorry, boys, but I draw the line there. No dogs." Chelsea shook her head.

"Can you watch the boys this afternoon? I'm meeting with the lawyer." I checked my watch, exhilaration coursing through me. I had dreamed of closing on the Maguire property.

The idea had struck me like lightning that day in the subway station on my way to the office. The platform was jammed tight with commuters. The train rushed through, bringing a gusty wind that lifted soot and debris and sent them flying throughout the platform. At that moment, I was somewhere else. I was that boy with the scraped knee, and Mary was gazing down at me. I had known then.

"Of course I will. We're going to make cookies. How about it, boys? Gingerbread?" She glared at the cardboard box.

"Where's Lincoln?" I tilted my head, wondering where my brother-in-law might be at this hour.

"He left early." She turned toward the dishwasher and pressed the start button.

"I didn't see him last night," I nudged. My sister worried me. Her marriage to Lincoln Frost had been sudden—too sudden. I recalled the phone call and her excitement traveling down the line. There was no time for invitations. The impromptu ceremony took place at the Hunt Club on the shores of the Pretty River on a frosty Christmas Eve one year ago this Christmas. I studied her profile, swallowed up in a red velvet robe.

"A meeting in the city." She glanced my way, her face pinched. "I don't understand why you bought that old place. You didn't even talk to me first."

"Chelsea, I can make my own decisions." She called the Maguire place a blight on the landscape.

I had to acknowledge she was right about that. The century-old house fulfilled a longing I hadn't been able to reach until now. After graduating from university, I returned to Forest Falls with one goal: to win over the girl I loved—Mary Christmas. When she rejected me, I left with no intention of coming back. I moved on. Ten years later, I returned—a single father with no clear plans for the future except to restore the old home and start anew with my boys.

"It should be condemned. Is it because of that Christmas woman? Tell me it's not because of her. Have you not been humiliated enough?" She huffed. "Would you boys like Auntie Chelsea's famous chocolate chip pancakes? Or how about raspberry waffles?

"What does 'hum-ill-ated' mean, Auntie Chelsea?" Dash shoveled another cookie into his mouth.

"Pancakes, pancakes." Alfie jumped from his stool and lunged toward Chelsea, wrapping his chubby arms around her waist and burying his face in her robe.

"Don't pay any attention to me, sweetie. Auntie Chelsea is just being silly." She looked down at Alfie, and her face crumpled. "Pancakes, it is. You can help me with the chocolate chips, okay?"

I looked at my sister, pondering my current situation. I had planned on renting suitable accommodation while the renovations were underway, but Chelsea insisted we stay. The house was big enough, with two rambling wings and a central family space, but what seemed like a temporary solution was becoming more of a challenge than I had anticipated. Moving into the new place couldn't come soon enough.

"Dad, can we get a dog? Please, Dad." Alfie begged for the eighty-fifth time since yesterday.

Chapter Three

Mary

I threw my arm sideways, stroking the still-sleeping Tinsel. How many years ago had I said goodbye to Christopher, and how many days since had I regretted that decision?

Images of him flooded my dreams: the sun-drenched afternoon, the sweet fragrance of roses. The memory of Christopher holding a bouquet of blue violets and white daisies is etched in my soul. He proposed to me on the front porch of my grandfather's farmhouse.

"I can't leave." Those were my exact words. I forgot the most crucial part—I loved him. The next day, hopeful me drove to the train station. I could only watch as the morning express left the station two minutes ahead of schedule, taking the love of my life with it. I could have called him. I could have gone after him. I did neither. He left without a backward glance, and part of me, the stupid part, never forgave him. What had I expected? What choice had I given him?

I buried my face in the pillow, squeezing my eyelids shut. He was so damn irresistible, with that goofy grin on his face, dressed in that silly polka-dot apron, and he smelled so damn good, and I turned him down—again. What was I so afraid of?

The rumbling of the snowblower's engine broke the morning's stillness.

The horses needed attending.

My shift at the mall started in five hours.

The wind whistled, shaking the windowpanes of the attic suite I called my own. A back staircase spilling into the kitchen, once used by the help in another era, separated the upper space from the main house. I added my personal touches: a four-piece bathroom, complete with a soaker tub, and over the king-sized bed, a skylight meant for stargazing. The sloping ceilings took some getting used to.

My phone chirped.

The bakery. Oh God.

—Mary, I can't make it this afternoon. Clarabel has the flu.—

"Sure, I can be in two places at once." I stared at my phone and sighed loud enough to wake Tinsel. I tapped my phone's keyboard, sending out the alarms.

"Come on, girlie. Let's go." I clambered from the bed, doing my best to avoid disturbing Tinsel, my feet sinking into the plush carpet.

Snow drifted in during the night, lacing the window-panes with an icy frost. I looked over the ancient spruce trees that lined the driveway at the herd of white-tailed deer sheltered beneath the laden boughs. In the distance, the Maguire homestead stood empty, with fifty acres of Scotch Pine and Balsam Fir abutting the abandoned farmhouse.

Open daily for the holiday season, Christmas's

Christmas Tree Farm gave families that chop-down-your-own tree in the Canadian North experience. Baling was free, saws were provided, and pre-cut trees were available for the less adventurous.

People asked how I ran this place on my own.

Staffing was not a concern. The elves from the North Pole called Christmas's Christmas Tree Farm their second home, a holiday from the Arctic North. The second-floor bedrooms were filled all summer, and the studio over the garage was held for the grand elf himself.

At this time of year, my helpers were scarce. More concerning was the upcoming arrival of Santa's sleigh, which would transport the elderly elf back to his workshop in preparation for the final flight of the year on Christmas Eve.

I shimmied into my stretchy jeans and dug through the stack of clothes piled on the armchair, still waiting for the laundry. I tossed tops and pants onto the floor, searching for my favorite sweatshirt—a thick fleece embroidered with a red-nosed reindeer.

The farmhouse, built on the sheltered slope of Christmas Mountain where the Pretty River idled on by, passed from generation to generation.

"Are you up?" I called out to Tinsel, who landed on the floor with a thump.

I brushed my teeth. I wiped down the counter, sweeping ponytail holders into the drawer. I brushed my hair and twisted the length into a French braid. What would happen to Santa and the elves if something happened to me? The clock was ticking in more ways than one.

I ran down the stairs, with Tinsel charging ahead. Old Nick would ring the doorbell any moment, and if the coffee was not ready and waiting, my name would go on the naughty list.

I punched the soundbox, blasting a rock and roll playlist through the country kitchen. I stretched high and then touched my toes, twisting my hips to the heavy backbeat.

Tinsel pranced. Standing on her hind legs, she twirled on the spot.

I stood at the counter, grinding coffee beans, inhaling the rich aroma of a chocolate and cranberry medley. I filled the water dispenser and pressed start—coffee on.

I slid sideways, singing my heart out to my favorite tune.

Tinsel threw her head upward and howled.

"Okay, that's enough. Good Girl." I threw her a venison jerky treat.

Like clockwork, the doorbell played a series of merry bells.

"Come in," I sang.

Tinsel barked, charging to greet the merry gent.

"Good morning, Mary." After stamping his black boots on the braided carpet, he hung his parka in the pine-paneled foyer and removed his cap, unveiling a head of shiny, snow-white waves secured with a leather thong. The white beard hugging his chin extended to his collarbone, and his cheerful lips were adorned with a neatly trimmed mustache.

"Coffee's on. Can I interest you in a croissant, Nick?" I gestured to the platter filled with pastries—day-olds from the bakery I retrieved the night before.

I turned away, filling Tinsel's bowl with kibble. Lady-bug, the orange cat, meowed and weaved between Tinsel's legs. I scooped tuna into her bowl.

"No, not today. We need to talk about sales." A wintry blast drifted along the floorboards, following him into the country kitchen. The straight-back wooden chair groaned as he lowered himself onto it.

"We do? Why? Is there a problem?" I grabbed the coffee pot, filling two oversized ceramic mugs, each glazed with animated images of the legendary figure himself.

"There is. Not enough families are coming by. I'm worried." He tapped plump fingers on the harvest table, deep lines etching his forehead.

"We still have a few days, Nick. It's never too late." I smiled hopefully.

"It's a frosty one today." He polished his spectacles against the soft fabric of his red fleece. "Might scare people away."

"I wouldn't worry, Nick. I saw the sack of letters you were working on last night." I placed a steaming mug before him.

"That's true. Lots of letters this year." He dropped four sugar cubes into his coffee and added a dollop of heavy cream.

People came from far and wide to experience a taste of Christmas magic by cutting down their holiday trees. Free hot chocolate enticed shoppers to pick up a bottle or two of maple syrup or a tub of wildflower honey, and the horse-drawn sleigh was the icing on the cake.

"I fear the magic is fading. There are fewer and fewer believers every year." He stirred his coffee, the spoon clanking against the mug.

"And you think that's related to the number of tree sales?" I nibbled my bottom lip, considering his worries.

"There's no doubt in my mind. It's concerning." He pinched his bushy eyebrows together.

"There's still the last-minute rush. I'm not worried," I reassured him, but a ripple of doubt remained.

"I hope you're right." His rosy cheeks dimpled when he smiled.

"You're flipping pancakes again this year. Mrs. Sandusky informed me." I smirked and raised one eyebrow—Nick's weakness—stacks of fluffy pancakes drizzled with homemade maple syrup.

"And then I'll be leaving, Mary. You'll be here alone till after Christmas." He peered over his spectacles.

"You're sweet to worry, Nick." I sipped the fragrant coffee.

"I can leave Jory to help out with the horses." He tilted his head, his pensive gaze hinting at more critical concerns. Jory spent more time on Christmas Mountain than any other elf.

"What? What is it?" I placed my hand over his leathered one.

"I heard the Maguire place sold. You do know what that means?" He looked at me with furrowed white brows.

"No, what does it mean?" On a clear day, the sun would glint off the slate roof of the old Maguire place, reflecting all seven rainbow shades. The place was magical, and I was surprised that others couldn't see it.

"It's a shame your grandfather never bought that land." He shook his head.

"Why?" I blew on my coffee, dispersing the steam.

"You know why, Mary. The elves, the reindeer, the sleigh, coming and going." He reached for a chocolate croissant.

"Christopher Northbrook bought the Maguire place, Nick. He's going to live there with his kids. There's nothing to worry about." I knew Christopher. His intentions were good, or were they? I considered the possibilities, the what-ifs.

"That's not true, Mary. Your magic keeps Christmas Mountain safe, and that magic doesn't extend beyond the far tree line. You know that." He took a tentative bite, golden flakes falling onto his beard.

I hadn't thought much about Maguires in the last few years. It never occurred to me that someone would buy the vacant parcel. I chewed on the inside of my mouth, realizing what a stroke of luck it was that it was Christopher and not some big-city developer.

Nick was right. Of course, he was right.

I looked inside my heart, and the magic stirred—the wind and snow, cloud and haze, followed me around this property, keeping Santa's secrets safe. I had only to raise my arms, and the earthly spirits would heed my call.

I discovered the magic as a young girl the day I glimpsed the most beautiful boy in the world, Christopher. It happened innocently enough.

I had climbed the branches of an oak tree high on the mountain slope, my favorite place in all the world. I sat up there for hours, lost in the pages of a book. He appeared out of nowhere. My heart fluttered, and the wind stirred. I almost lost my grip when the branches whipped from side to side, tossing acorns onto the ground. He had yelled at me to stop.

That was when the magic found me.

I stared at the fireplace, my eyes resting on the framed photo of the little man posing with my grandfather's grandfather—Cooper Kringle, the ageless elf who orchestrated Santa's sleigh's first visit to the Forest Falls.

When the wind whispered, and the moon drifted behind the clouds, nine reindeer would land in the hollow, and the shining sleigh would glide to a silent stop. The reindeer were fed, watered, and kept overnight in the barn. At the same time, the elves packed the sleigh with much-needed whatsits and thingamabobs—everything needed to restock Santa's workshop. Thanks to Aredhel, who organized and sourced each order and arranged delivery to Christmas Mountain.

Once in a blue moon, the nearby airport's radar would pick up an anomaly and send someone to investigate. They would leave confused and touched with a healthy dose of Christmas magic.

That was the thing. When people arrived at Christmas's Christmas Tree Farm, magic touched them. When they left, they took a small piece of it with them. In some, it blossomed—in others, it faded away.

I gathered the two coffee mugs while Nick reached for a candy cane croissant.

"I'll be off now." He lumbered to the front door and shrugged into his coat.

Tinsel followed the trail of candy crystals, lapping each one with her pink tongue.

"I'll be out shortly, Nick." I placed the mugs in the dishwasher and gazed out the window into the side yard.

Jory wore a four-pointed green felt hat that covered his pointed ears. Tall for an elf, he moved back and forth between Molly and Big, adjusting the rigging and checking the harnesses. He stroked their broad faces and fed them both a carrot. I watched him run his hand down their muscular legs over their silky feathers. The horses nudged him affectionately, anticipating the day's first hayride.

I wiped my hands on the dish towel, picked up a red marker, and crossed out today's date on the wall calendar. Two more days remained until the sleigh arrived, restocking the last gizmos and gadgets and taking Nick and Jory back to the Arctic Circle.

For the first time, I was worried about the future. What if I could no longer keep them safe?

* * *

A line of people ran down the street outside the bakery, with only twenty minutes left until closing. The door opened and closed with every customer, the jingling bell announcing the latest arrival. The last customer of the day was Chelsea Frost, looking smart in a red woolen pea coat and tailored black trousers. A furry black hat concealed her curled locks.

"That's twenty-six dollars and ninety-eight cents. Would you like a bag?" I looked over the cash register, meeting Chelsea's wide smile. "They're one dollar, and the money raised each week goes to the food bank."

"Yes, of course, please. I have to tell you. These gingerbread cookies are wonderful. When Christopher brought them home yesterday, they were gone in a snap. I tried making them." She giggled. "They were awful, Mary. I had to toss them into the trash. So here I am." She tapped her credit card on the point-of-sale device.

Holiday cheer? Christmas magic? I gazed at her, lost for words, and then recovered.

"Oh, I'm glad. I'm glad you liked the cookies, I mean." I passed the paper tote across the counter.

"Goodbye, and have a lovely day." She waved and walked out the door, stopping on the sidewalk. "Darlene, it's nice to see you. You must pick up some of these gingerbread cookies. They are just magical."

I stared after her, dumbfounded. I looked at my hands and the cookies. It couldn't be. No way.

"Holy moly, what's gotten into her?" JoJo shifted her

head sideways, her gaze following Chelsea. She twirled the feather duster over the glass cabinets, landing in a fencing stance.

I shot her a glance and carried on. After five more orders, I wished the final Merry Christmas of the night.

"Can you lock up? I have to get out of here." I tossed JoJo the keys and headed toward the back alley where my car waited.

"Hey, wait. You didn't tell me. What's happening with the hottie? Is something going on?" JoJo threw her hands to her heart-shaped face and did a two-step dance sideways, clicking her heels on the tile floor. I could not ignore the hopeful grin on her face.

"Oh, JoJo. My life is a mess. I don't know what to do." I bent at the waist, tugging slouchy biker boots onto my feet.

"Tell him. For God's sake, now is your chance. He's back, and he wants you. That's frickin' obvious." She clapped her hands together.

"It's not that simple, JoJo." I swept my hands over my hips, smoothing the oversized sweater, the canary-yellow knit embroidered with an orange rubber ducky.

"Umm, yeah. It is. You're the problem, girlfriend. Get over it. Tell him you love him. You've always loved him. You want to take him home and make babies. Yeah, that's right! Two or three of them, at least." She removed her round glasses and crossed her eyes on purpose.

"Don't do that. You're not supposed to do that." I huffed and threw an apron at her. "I'll see you later." I turned to leave but then stopped. "I love you, JoJo. Thank you."

"Yeah, anytime." She flicked the edge of the apron in my direction and smiled. "Hey, I love the sweater."

Chapter Four

Christopher

Brocklebank Law exuded classic charm, with rich wood-paneled walls and age-old barrister bookcases polished to a golden hue. I sat in a leather high-back chair, my feet flat on the floor, and looked around the office. Jared's diploma hung proudly next to a series of framed photos brought to life through his camera's lens. Captivating images featured local wildlife, including a mother bear with three cubs, a red fox stalking its prey, and a raccoon nestled in a tree. The photos added warmth to an otherwise professional atmosphere.

"Congratulations, Chris. The town of Forest Falls is fortunate to have you back." Jared was a partner at his father's law firm, grounded in small-town life. I envied him.

"Thanks, man. I'm happy to be here." I grinned at my high school pal, the lawyer responsible for closing the sale of the Maguire property.

"It's nice to see someone tackling that old place. It's been empty for far too long. I hope you're up for the challenge."

He reached over the wide desk, handing me the deed and a few keys dangling from a silver ring.

"Me, too." I chuckled. "Nice photos, bud." I crossed the office floor and sifted through the array of unframed shots scattered across an empty desk. I studied each one with an untrained eye.

"Thanks. I'm heading to Diamond Mine on the weekend if the weather cooperates. There's a nest of bald eagles on the highest peak." He grinned, his eyes catching fire with excitement.

"That's a good hike. Isn't that where we camped out with Pencil and Moose?" I referred to our mutual buddies from grade school. I had lost touch with so many good guys, real friends.

"Yeah, man. That's the one." He rose from behind the desk and extended his hand. "Let's catch up soon."

"I'd like that." I clasped his palm and shook hands, making a promise I intended to keep.

"Hold on. I have something for you." He turned to a tall filing cabinet and rifled through the top drawer, removing a yellowed envelope. "I found these in the historical records. I thought you'd like them."

"Thanks, man." I flipped through the grainy photographs. "That's amazing."

"Hey, no worries. Aredhel will see you out." Jared looked sideways, his eyes softening as a tall woman entered his office.

"It's nice to see you again, Christopher. Welcome back." She greeted me with a half-smile, her long blonde hair cascading over her shoulder.

"Thanks." I nodded, wondering when we had met. I couldn't recall seeing her before. She had the most extraordinary eyes and a fashion sense that fit the big city better than little Forest Falls.

"Have a lovely evening." She ducked her head, motioning toward the exit, and closed the door with a soft click.

I glanced over my shoulder, an eerie sensation flowing through me.

As I signed the final documents, day had turned into night. I patted my inside pocket, ensuring the keys remained secure.

Forest Falls awakened something inside me. I gazed into the dark velvet sky, awed by a carpet of twinkling stars. Mary's face flitted through my mind, the curve of her lips when she smiled.

I looked beyond the carousel at the festival of lights illuminating the riverside park. A couple, hands entwined, stopped before a life-sized candle shimmering in iridescent blue, its orange flame brilliant against the night. Cheek to cheek, they beamed at a selfie stick. I averted my gaze, feeling like an intruder.

"Hey, look where you're going." She slammed into me— or did I slam into her?

I looked up and found Mary flat on her bottom, her bare legs stretched out on the sidewalk. I stood, frozen in place, as her shopping bag tipped sideways, spilling shiny red apples beyond her short boots and into the gutter.

"I wasn't looking. I'm so sorry. Are you all right?" I jumped forward, slipping my hands beneath her elbows and hoisting her onto her feet. "Are you hurt?" I gripped her shoulders, my hands sinking into the fluffy down of a hooded bomber jacket fringed with faux fur. I gazed into those lovely eyes.

"I'm fine." Her eyes twinkled. Or were they stars in my

eyes? She placed one hand on my chest, backing away from our embrace. "Maybe slightly bruised." She glanced at the apples.

"I'm sorry." I reached for her bag, recovering each slush-covered apple, three from the sidewalk and six from the gutter.

"Thanks." She removed her mittens, shaking each, sending icy droplets everywhere.

"Let me replace these, yeah?" I gazed at the sloppy mess inside the shopping bag.

"The market's closed." She nodded toward the corner grocery and the closed sign hanging in the window.

"Tomorrow?" I looked hopeful.

"Where were you, Christopher? You seemed far away." Her voice softened, and she smiled.

"I was." I reached into my pocket and displayed the handful of keys. "It's official."

"Oh wow. Congratulations. You always loved that place." Her face lit up.

"Celebrate with me. How about it, yeah? An evening of holiday cheer?" I grinned, hoping for the answer I sought.

"Um, I'm not sure." She shrugged.

"Come on, where else do you need to be?" I touched her elbow.

"Well, that's presumptuous of you." She bent sideways, brushing slush from the back of her yellow sweater. Her lips rose into a crooked smile. "A glass of wine, maybe?"

"Sure. Where would you like to go?" I looked down the main street, realizing there were more food places than anything else.

"The Gnome? I heard they have great craft brews." She gestured toward the opposite corner, where a neon sign of a red-hatted gnome hung above an arched doorway.

I placed my hand on the small of her back, guiding her across the road, ensuring no further mishaps occurred. We stood on the sidewalk while a crowd exited the restaurant, carrying the fragrant scents of hops and barley onto the street.

"This is cool." I admired the spacious interior.

Once the town's timber mill, a dynamic entrepreneur converted the warehouse into a gathering place with hanging lights, reclaimed timber floors, high-sided booths, and tables lacquered to a golden sheen.

"Welcome to The Gnome." The hostess greeted us at the door. "A table for two?"

"Yes, please." I spotted an old-fashioned jukebox in a corner, surrounded by a well-worn dance floor. "Do you come here often?"

"Me? No. Not really." She blushed.

The server ushered us toward a window seat overlooking the park.

"Perfect, thank you." I nodded.

"Your server will be here shortly. Enjoy." She left us alone in the grand hall.

"Here, let me help." I slid her coat from her shoulders and hung it on an ornately carved hook beside the booth. Butterflies danced in my stomach. I wanted to wrap my arms around her, which would be inappropriate—too many years had passed.

She slid into the booth and sat straight-shouldered, her hands folded, the long sleeves of her sweater reaching her first knuckle.

"You look nice." I smiled, admiring the loose knit.

"Yellow is my color." She smirked. "It makes my eyes pop, don't you think?"

"You'd look beautiful in anything." I sat on the opposite

bench, my hands on my lap. The last thing I wanted to do was scare her away. Tasting her lovely lips was not an option—not yet.

"Oh, stop." She tugged on her sleeves.

"Hi there, folks." The server offered menu boards.

"Thank you." Mary greeted the server with a sparkling smile.

"Beverages to start?" The server inquired.

"Sure. What's on tap?" I rested my fingers on the menu.

"We have several craft brews, but I recommend Santa's Helper. It's a dark beer with a frothy head aged in a bourbon barrel. It features chocolate, figs, and nutmeg notes, with a subtle hum and moderate carbonation." The server nodded.

"Santa's Helper? I can't say no to that. Mary, how about you?" I grinned.

"I'll have the mulled wine, please." She peered over the rim of the menu board.

"Of course. The cinnamon?" The server asked.

"Yes, please." She lifted her eyebrows.

"Excellent choice." The server said.

"Should we look at the menu?" I met Mary's gaze.

"I can't stay long." Her face flushed a pretty shade of pink.

"Are you hungry? What about an appetizer?" I scanned the entries.

"Christopher." Her half-smile enchanted me.

"Burrata salad? Chicken wings?" I coaxed, recalling her favorites.

She twirled her hair into a long twist and looked at me.

"Hey, look what I have. Old photos of the Maguire place." I dug through my inside pocket and tapped the envelope on the table.

"Photos? Really?" She leaned in.

I slipped the envelope open, revealing five black-and-white photographs: nighttime shots of the century-old home basking in the moon's glow.

"Wow, where did you get these?" She studied each photo, shooting me a glance. "Jared took these?"

"No. They were leftovers from the Heritage Society. He thought I'd like to have them." I looked up as the server arrived.

"Here we are, folks. Cinnamon Mulled Wine for you, Miss, and Santa's Helper for the gentleman." The server set paper coasters adorned with dancing gnomes on the table, followed by each drink.

"Thank you. And we'll share the Charcuterie Board, please." I nodded, my gaze resting on Mary.

"Wonderful. I'll get that going for you guys." The server reached for the menus, taking them with her as she walked away.

Mary reached for her glass but knocked it over with her thumb. When the glass toppled onto the table, she jumped. "Oh, no. Christopher, I'm so sorry." Her eyes widened at the wave of Sangria flooding across the snapshots and spilling over the table's edge.

"Here, let me." I grabbed my napkin, sopping up what I could. "Excuse me, Miss. Could we get more napkins?"

"Oh dear, of course. Of course." The server set a thick stack before us. "Allow me to get you another glass, ma'am."

"Thank you. That would be lovely." Mary finished soaking up the spill and handed the sodden napkins to the server.

"Well, where were we?" I met her stark gaze.

"Christopher, I'm sorry." She dipped her shoulders, then gathered the ruined photographs into a sticky stack.

"Hey, it's not a big deal." I smiled, nodding at the bag of bruised apples. "We're even now."

She slid the stained photos into the envelope, placing the entire mess into her shopping bag.

"Here we are, Cinnamon Sangria." The server returned with a tall glass adorned with a cinnamon stick. "And a starter of deep-fried pickles on the house. Again, I'm so sorry for the mishap."

"Oh, thank you so much. That wasn't necessary. It was my fault." Mary's face flushed pink.

"Not to worry, folks." The server walked away.

"Hmm, these are pretty good." I bit into one golden pickle.

"So is this. Want to try it?" She sipped her drink.

"No. No thanks." I observed her stiff posture. "Don't worry about the photos. It's not important."

"How are your folks doing?" She played with the ribbed cuff of her sweater.

"Well, Dad keeps busy in his garden. Mom's writing her romance novels. They love Mexico." I grinned, shaking my head.

"Nice." She seemed distant.

I needed to bring her back to me.

"Can I ask you a question?" She took another sip of her drink, studying me.

"Of course. Anything." I tasted the cold brew, savoring the festive flavors.

"What happened to Isabelle?" She placed her fingers on mine and asked in a quiet voice.

I realized she would ask. We were once inseparable, sharing everything—there was even a time when I could read her thoughts. That bond came to an abrupt end when I left her behind.

"Isabelle died in a multi-car pile-up on her way to work." I shared the devastating news from that fateful morning.

"That must have been difficult." Her gaze didn't waver.

"It was. I've had a long time to process and move my life forward. It's important for the boys, you know?" I accepted the loss a long time ago.

She stared into my soul and nodded, her wavy locks tumbling over her shoulder.

"It's been quite a while since I've done this." I played with her fingers, hope flickering in my heart. The lump lodged in my throat was not sadness. It was hunger and need for the woman I walked away from. How could I have been so blind? What I would give to run my fingers through those silken waves.

"What? Knock somebody on their ass?" She smirked and then laughed, lighting up the room.

"Sit in a quiet booth with a beautiful woman." I caressed her thumb with mine.

A glass broke, smashing onto the floor. A fifties tune blared from the jukebox. Voices intertwined with laughter. My gaze remained fixed on Mary.

"It's been a while for me, as well." She dipped her head and watched me through strawberry gold eyelashes.

The server placed the charcuterie between us, and another provided cutlery and serving plates. I shifted in my seat, tamping down my hunger.

"Wow, thank you." She smiled.

"How about a toast?" I tipped my glass toward hers. "To us. To the future."

"Christopher, there is no 'us.'" She leaned back in the booth, distancing herself and erecting an impenetrable wall.

"Let me change that." I looked into those fiery eyes. She challenged me at every turn.

"You don't know what you're saying." She huffed and reached for a cube of gouda cheese.

"Give me a chance. We can go as slow as you want." I placed my hands flat on the table, sensing her need for space.

"There are things you don't know about me." She chewed slowly.

"What things would that be?" Something mysterious hid behind her smile. I intended to unravel her secrets.

"You wouldn't understand. It's something I would have to show you." She looked away, scanning the faces entering the restaurant.

"I'm intrigued." I drew on the beer mug.

She looked sideways and then toward me. She leaned across the table in a conspiratorial manner. "Do you believe in Santa Claus?"

"Of course. Who doesn't?" I chuckled.

"I'm serious. Do you believe in Santa Claus? The Elves. The North Pole." A line appeared on her forehead.

"That's childhood fantasy, don't you think?" I pressed my lips together, hiding my laughter. This was the secret she wanted to share. I sat back against the bench. When was the last time I truly believed?

"Not even a little?" She touched my hand.

I clenched my fists, struck by an unexpected jolt. The night sky shimmered with stars. She was the brightest among them, distant and unattainable—I longed to be with her.

Sparking neurons awakened memories long buried. I reached for each one, seeing sharp details in vivid technicolor.

I was seven years old, and it was Christmas Eve. I had awoke from a deep sleep, hearing a clatter on the rooftop and a heavy thud on the living room floor. I crept down the stairs and froze, barely breathing, as I peered through the stair railings. Santa stood in the center of the living room, his red velvet suit, fringed with white snow glimmered in soft light, rummaging through a bottomless red sack. He padded back and forth, his footsteps silent. Wonder filled my mind, my heart bursting with happiness—I saw him with my own eyes—Santa Claus, that jolly old elf. When I shared my exciting news in the morning, my mother told me it was all a wonderful dream.

"Are you going to eat any of this?" She nibbled on a grape, distant and unreadable.

"Where did you go?" I inhaled a sharp, icy breath, chills racing down my spine.

"I didn't go anywhere, Christopher. You did." A small smile lit up her eyes.

"I don't understand." My memories were mere wisps, fragments of a time lost. A black curtain crashed down, closing the door.

"This is good. You should try some." She spread sour cherry preserves over a slice of cheddar.

My mind spun. I cut through the fog, grasping at the memory that had slipped away like a snowflake floating through the night sky.

"Einstein? Is that you, man?" Donny Taylor loomed large, occupying all available space in the narrow aisle. As tall as he was and just as wide, had earned him the nickname Big Tree in seventh grade.

"Big Tree. Pencil. Hey, this is awesome." I rose from the booth, wrapping two grown men in a bear hug.

"Hey, man." Stan Corner, aka the Pencil, punched my forearm with a heavy fist.

"He's back, boys. And he's moving into the old Maguire

place." She twined her hands together and wiggled in her seat.

They noticed Mary as if for the first time. Pencil's face reddened. Big Tree elbowed me. Some things always stayed the same.

"Hi, Donny. How's Beth?" She smiled, unaware of his discomfort.

"Just fine. Thanks for asking." He grinned sheepishly and then looked at me. "You got your gear with you, bro? We need you real bad, man."

"Hockey?" I lifted my chin. I had yet to play since leaving Forest Falls so many years ago.

"Yeah, man. It's the annual Pond Hockey Tournament." Pencil joined the conversation. Silent by nature, he earned the nickname with his ability to 'erase' his opponents on the ice.

"Pond hockey? When did we play pond hockey?" I looked at Mary for the answer.

"Philp's Pond, by the water tower." She nodded.

"It's a tradition, man—Forest Falls vs. Beacon Hill. The winner takes the Giant Candy Cane. We've held the title for the last three years. Say yes, man." Big Tree's grin spread from ear to ear.

"I haven't played in years." I made excuses. It's not that I wouldn't play.

"We need you, bro. Boothy broke his ankle, snow blowing his driveway. Bad luck for him." Big Tree shook his head from side to side.

"We're in a pinch, Einstein. Hey? You got kids? There's a family skate after the game. Bonfire. Hot dogs." Pencil hovered in the aisle, calling me by a nickname I hadn't heard in years.

"When is it?" I grinned. I'd forgotten what it was to have friends.

"Two o'clock, day after tomorrow. Full gear. Bring your 'A' game."

"Full gear? For pond hockey?"

"We got goalies and a ref. It's the real deal." Pencil pounded his fist against his chest in reverence to the game.

"I wouldn't miss it for the world." I grinned.

"Does Beans know you're in town? He'll be stoked." Pencil nodded his head.

"Hey, why don't you and Mary join us for a few brews? The guys should be here any minute. You remember Mulch and Chin?" Big Tree pointed toward a long harvest table filling the center aisle.

"Thanks, guys, but..." My gaze returned to Mary.

"Go ahead, I was just leaving." She slipped from the booth before I could object.

My heart dropped. I had hoped the evening would unfold differently, but the image of a romantic walk along the river faded away.

"Don't leave, Mary." Big Tree's gaze darted back and forth.

"Great seeing you, Mary." Pencil acknowledged her with a nod, taking her place in the booth. He reached for a handful of grapes, popping them into his mouth one by one.

"Hey, no worries. Looks like you have a lot of catching up to do." She reached for her jacket.

"Do you still have that dog, Mary? What was her name?" Big Tree's crooked smile was almost endearing.

"Will you bear witness to my return to the arena?" I held her coat while she slipped into it.

"It's a pond, Christopher. Not an arena." She turned,

flipping her hair over her shoulders. I breathed in her scent, and my knees almost buckled.

"Say yes, Mary." Big Tree and Pencil chimed in harmony.

She pinned her bottom lip beneath her pretty white teeth and surveyed us with twinkling eyes.

"Say yes, Mary." I lifted her hand, pressed my lips to her knuckles, and held my breath. Touching her made my head spin.

"Woot. Woot. Woot." Big Tree slammed his fist, spilling Sangria on the table.

"You got the moves, Einstein, I'll give you that." Pencil swallowed three cubes of gouda.

"I'd love to watch you play hockey." She slung her shopping bag over her shoulder.

"Until then, Mary Christmas." I dipped my head, pressing my lips to her cheek. "I will dream of you, my love."

Her breath hitched, and her face turned pink. She hesitated and then turned away.

My heart soared.

"Bye, Mary." Pencil winked at me.

Big Tree slid into the booth, pushing Pencil into the corner.

I turned toward my buddies, joining them for what I knew would be an evening of laughs and probably a sore head in the morning.

Chapter Five

Mary

Big fat snowflakes floated down from a grey sky, enveloping the merry-go-round in an enchanting world of falling snow. The carousel looked like postcard picture or a snowglobe, the kind I would shake as a child, imagining the world within. Tinsel nudged my fingers, communicating her wishes.

"All right, but you stay there. Don't wander off." I left her beside the carousel, where she worked magic with every child she met.

The smoky aroma of maple syrup drifted in the frosty air. My mouth watered, anticipating the first mouthful of Old Nick's pancakes—perfectly browned with crispy edges, topped with a dollop of whipped butter. I followed my nose to the Forest Falls Community Pavilion, decked with heart-red baubles and swathed in fragrant cedar boughs.

"Mary! Would you like to buy a ticket for a Holiday Center-piece? Twenty-five lucky winners will take home one of our lovely arrangements. Three for five dollars, dear." Mrs. Sandusky nodded her greyed head at the festive bouquets adorning every other table. I followed her gaze, taking in baskets stuffed with feathery boughs bursting with berry-laden sprigs.

"Yes, please." I handed her five dollars and stuck the numbered tickets in my coat pocket.

"Hot cocoa, ma'am?" The teenager held a tray of steaming paper cups wrapped in red and green napkins.

"Hmm, thank you." I wrapped my hands around the warm paper cup.

Another volunteer rang a bell, drawing attention to the Christmas Kettle filled with paper bills. I slipped twenty dollars into the kettle and joined the long line waiting for pancakes. Thankfully, the line moved quickly.

"Especially for you." Nick's blue eyes glowed bright. He slid two fluffy pancakes onto a paper plate and handed them to me.

"It's tonight, then?" I studied his complexion. His cheeks were rosier than the day before—a telltale sign the sleigh would arrive with the rising moon.

"It seems so. It seems so." He flipped one pancake after another onto the sizzling grill, then looked up and gave me a wink.

"It's a perfect day, isn't it, Mary?" Chelsea's soprano voice reached everyone in the room.

I glanced over my shoulder and met her gaze. Her face was pale, and her eyes were ringed with dark circles.

"Chelsea, Lincoln, it's nice to see you both." I could not ignore her pained expression. She seemed more than distraught. It was not like Chelsea to wear her heart on her sleeve.

"It's good to see you, Mary." Lincoln smiled. "Will you

be joining us for the Holiday skate this afternoon?" Two pairs of skates hung over the shoulder of his black parka.

"Skating? Oh, I've never been much of a skater, Lincoln." I grinned.

"Keep the line moving." A young man barked from the back.

"Lincoln is giving his holiday speech today. I hope you can make it." She gently touched my arm, urging my attendance.

"Oh, I wouldn't miss it." The Mayor's annual Christmas message spread optimism and joy to Forest Falls's constituents. This was a big day in Forest Falls.

"Nick, do you know Chelsea? And her husband, Lincoln." I rested my gaze on Lincoln Frost. The man always seemed so preoccupied.

Nick reached over the counter, handing off two plates of fragrant pancakes.

"Yes, I do. I remember Chelsea Northbrook. How are you, young lady?" His bushy brows pinched together when he smiled. He handed Chelsea a stacked plate, his gaze drifting toward Lincoln. "And you, young man. I hope you brought your appetite." Nick looked over the rim of his spectacles.

"You can count on me, sir." He pressed forward with his hand resting on the elbow of Chelsea's baby blue belted onesie.

"Have you, by chance, seen my brother?" Chelsea tilted her fur-covered head and pinned her lips into a worried line.

"Merry Christmas, Mr. Mayor." Mr. Sandusky slapped Lincoln on the shoulder as he passed by.

"Christopher? No. No, I haven't. Why?" She had my attention.

"Oh, Mary. He moved the boys into that old house. I was so looking forward to having them stay for Christmas." Her voice rose in pitch, and her eyes glistened.

From middle grade onward, Chelsea was part of the 'in-crowd,' and I was Mary Christmas, the butt of Chelsea's jokes. To say there was any love lost between us would be a lie. Still, her remorseful tone caused concern.

"Honey, it's not your fault. He's your brother. You know what he's like." Lincoln wrapped his arm around her waist, pressing his lips onto her forehead.

"It is Lincoln." Her face crumbled. "He'll never forgive me."

"Help yourself, folks. Compliments to Christmas's Christmas Tree Farm." Nick motioned to the jugs of maple syrup, his voice booming.

Lincoln nodded and guided his wife toward an empty picnic table.

I dawdled at the counter's end, pouring syrup puddles onto my plate, focusing on the couple. Lincoln ate like a man possessed while Chelsea gazed furtively around the hall, leaving her pancakes untouched.

I shook my head, acknowledging the obvious. When Chelsea mentioned his name, my heart jolted. When I closed my eyes, I saw his face—last night had only heightened my desire and worry.

When I returned home, I dumped the contents of my shopping bag onto the kitchen table, my gaze falling on the photos. They captured the place before the happenings began—when the house was first built. My grandfather told me the eerie tale his father had shared with him. He had warned the Maguires not to make a home in that location, but they didn't listen.

I had studied each photo, with Christopher oblivious to

my rising alarm. The house was the focal point in the image, but when I looked carefully—I couldn't unsee it. Basked in the moon's glow, a dark shape flew through the sky. The sleigh. Santa's sleigh. Clear as day if you looked. Panic filled my mind even now. How many people might have seen those photos? Had Jared realized what he possessed?

I knocked my drink over in proper Mary fashion, soaking the images in dark red wine, rendering them unrecognizable. I stuffed the photos into my shopping bag to ensure they weren't shared. When I returned home, I had thrown them into the fireplace and watched as they caught fire and burned to ash.

I found an empty table near the door where I could monitor Tinsel. As much as I trusted her not to wander off, I was still worried. The wind had picked up in the last few minutes, lifting the snow and sending it sideways. I washed the last bite of pancakes down with my cold, hot chocolate.

"Mary?" His silken voice caressed my mind, and I wondered if I was dreaming.

He rested his hands on my shoulders, squeezed gently, and then slipped into the bench seat.

"Hi." He smiled that crooked smile.

"You made it." I cut into the last pancake.

"Pancakes in the park during a snowstorm. I wouldn't miss this for the world." He looked into the fast-falling snow. "It's a winter wonderland. Nothing like the slop we see in the city."

"Do you miss it?" I studied him.

"The city? Not at all. I was away too long." His voice filled with a rugged determination I wasn't used to hearing.

"Did you have fun with the guys?" My gaze swept over his messy hair and chin, stubbled with rich growth.

"I was sorry our evening ended so soon. But yes, it was great—just like old times." He grinned.

I weighed my words.

"You realize the Maguire place..." I cocked my head. He had to know.

"Is haunted? I don't believe in ghosts, Mary." He chuckled.

"Strange things happen there. It's something else. That's why the Maguires left." I dipped my chin, looking into his laughing eyes.

"I guess that's why I got it so cheap, yeah?" He chuckled.

"I didn't know it was for sale." I considered his recent purchase. "How did you get a hold of the owners, by the way?"

"Jared did some digging. The Estate of Esther Maguire held title to the property. The executor proved easy to find." He almost purred with excitement.

"Jared?" I gazed at him.

"Yeah, and his clerk. What was her name? Aredhel? She went above and beyond to track down the executor." He looked pleased with himself.

"Aredhel?" No. No. No. Aredhel, of all people, knew how important the Christmas secret was. My stomach rose in my throat.

"Yeah, that's her name. I think Jared has a thing for her." He chuckled. "We prepared an offer, and the executor accepted my bid." He folded his hands on the table, his facial muscles relaxing.

"Hmm. I don't know. There's a reason no one wanted to buy it." I reiterated my concern, but it was too late. Obviously.

"I'm not worried." He grinned. "And I'm ready for the challenge. I can't wait to turn the old place around."

"And then what?" I asked. I had to ask.

"And then what?" He looked at me with curiosity in his eyes.

"Are you going to sell it?" I needed to know, to hear it from him. Did he intend to stay? Was this merely a pit stop on his life journey? Is that what I was?

"I told you, didn't I? A big house with a yard where the boys can have a dog. Where we can be happy." He placed his fingers over mine. "That is my wish."

"Your sister's looking for you," I gestured toward Chelsea. "She seems upset. Maybe you should kiss and make up?" I lifted my brows.

"There's only one woman I long to kiss, and that woman is you." His voice crept beneath my skin, caressing my soul.

"Don't say that." Rising, I threw my empty plate into the trash can and left the pavilion with Christopher on my heels.

"Why not? It's true. Don't leave. Talk to me." He clasped my elbow, walking with me along the cobbled path.

"We are talking." I could barely discern the riverbank. I gazed at the wall of snow, at heavy flakes falling unabated and showing no signs of letting up. The carousel, hidden behind the white storm, sang its merry tune. "Where are the boys?" I wondered aloud.

"They're on the blue horses. I can see them from here." He led me down the cobblestone path. "Do you know what I dream of? More than anything in the world?"

"Um, no." I pulled up my zipper and rearranged my toque, wet flakes clinging to my eyelashes.

"To steal you away and let you have your way with me." He lifted my chin with the back of his knuckle, his eyes sparkling.

I swallowed the lump lodged in my throat. Was he reading my mind?

"Your sister is distraught." I clasped his wrist and looked him in the eye.

"And so she should be." His smirk revealed everything. "We had a 'disagreement.' Or should I say she disagreed?"

"She's your sister. Make things better." I gazed into the storm, now a full-on white-out, worried about tonight's arrival.

"She can stew a little longer." With his other hand, he brushed snowflakes from my hat.

"You're enjoying this, aren't you?" I smiled at him. For real, this time.

"It's about time someone disagreed with Chelsea Frost." He brushed his thumb over my bottom lip, whispering over me. Sparks flew between us—undeniable, fiery sparks.

"You're bad." I touched his cheek, loving how his stance had changed and his eyes had darkened.

"Let me show you how bad I can be." He lifted my fingers, pressing his lips to my knuckles.

"Christopher." How long had I dreamt of a moment like this? How long had I loved him?

Unseen, wrapped in winter's breath, he dragged his luscious lips down my face—a seductive play if there ever was one.

Heat shot through me, settling deep in my core. My mouth watered.

And then he cupped the back of my neck and claimed my mouth, parting my lips with the tip of his tongue. His scent filled my senses—bayberry, pine, and rich leather.

I welcomed him, battling his tongue, flicking the roof of his mouth, tasting the love I had lost.

"I want what we had, Mary. I want it back." He glided

his thumb along my jaw, tilting my face to receive him again. He brushed his tongue against mine, a slow dance of pleasure, a promise of so much more. His kiss was slow and relentless, touching every part of my soul.

I sank into the hard press of packed muscle and greedily opened for him, quickening and softening all at the same time, the voice of reason leaving me. He was all I ever wanted.

A dog barked. Children's laughter floated on a gust of wind.

"You don't know what you're saying." I pushed away, resting my hands on his shoulders and gazing into his beautiful face. He was so much the same, and yet I was not. "I'm not that girl, and you're not that boy. That was a lifetime ago."

"That's where you're wrong. We are those people—those same people. We're soulmates, Mary." His voice was breathless and raspy, tinged with molten heat.

"That's presumptuous of you, don't you think?" Too much had happened. Too much I couldn't explain or take back.

"Tell me it's not true? Tell me you don't feel the same." He caught my hands, pressing his lips onto the crown of my head.

He had stolen my heart many years ago. I could not deny my hunger for him. That didn't mean we had a future.

Tinsel's bark tore my attention away. Through the white squall, a dark shadow barreled toward me. She butted her heavy head into my hips, knocking me sideways.

"Tinsel, what is it?" I ran my hand through her silver ruff.

She took my hand in her jaws and pulled me into the

deep snow, prancing from side to side, yipping with urgency.

"Something's wrong." I jerked my head toward Tinsel.

"What are you trying to say?" The color drained from his face.

"What is it, Tinsel? Show me." I held onto her collar, letting her guide me.

"I don't see Alfie." He scanned the flying horses and the golden chariots.

"What? Where are they?" I glanced in the carousel's direction, realization crashing over me.

Tinsel whimpered, bent on her path toward the riverbank.

Christopher raced ahead and disappeared into the spinning carousel. He returned with one boy but not the other.

"He doesn't know where Alfie is." Fear played in his eyes, but he contained it. He knelt in front of the little boy. "Dash, where is your brother? Where did he go?"

"He wanted to go skating." Dash waved his hand into the flurry.

"When? When did he leave?" Christopher's voice hitched.

"It's okay, Christopher. I'm sure he's okay." My throat thickened. I wasn't sure of anything.

"I shouldn't have left them alone. What was I thinking?" He blamed himself.

"Daddy." The little boy pressed his face against his father's chest, tears flowing in wet rivulets down his chubby cheeks.

"It's okay, Dash. We'll find him. I promise." He hugged the little boy tight.

"Stay here, okay? In case Alfie comes back." I placed my hand on his arm.

"I can't just stay here." His anguish broke my heart.

The wind whistled, stinging my face. I held my hand over my eyes.

"You have to. The storm is getting worse. If you leave, Alfie won't find you. Stay here. Let me go with Tinsel." I said in a loud voice, convincing myself.

Tinsel whined and barked again.

"Go, Tinsel. Find." I set Tinsel free. She bolted down the path, lengthening her stride, veering onto the skating trail, weaving through figures coated in white. I ran beside the trail, my feet pounding through the packed snow.

I quelled the panic rising in my heart, fighting the 'what ifs' flying through my mind. If the child went toward the river and fell into the frigid water—a little boy would be no match for the raging current.

Up ahead, a lone boy with his arms outstretched and dressed in an orange snowsuit broke through the white wall, gliding sideways on the ice trail. His laughter rang out, reminding me of the silver bells on Santa's sleigh. He fell on his bottom and then hopped onto his feet.

"Alfie," I called his name, my breath hitching.

Tinsel lunged, grabbing the boy's snowsuit and holding him by his orange hood.

Relief flowed over me, and I dropped to my knees on the hard ice. "Alfie, do you know who I am? And Tinsel, do you remember her?"

Tinsel whined and licked the boy's face. He laughed and lifted his hand, patting Tinsel's ruff.

"Your dad is searching for you. Can you come with me?" I took his hand in mine.

"I'm not allowed to leave with strangers unless they know the magic words." His gaze narrowed, and then he laughed at Tinsel.

"The magic words?" The snow lessened, and the sun broke through the clouds.

"Yep." He buried his face in Tinsel's fur.

Skaters weaved around us: a little boy, a grown woman, and a dog. I pondered my predicament—magic words. What in the world could it be? And then it came to me, in lightning bolt fashion...

"Sugarplum. Lollipop." I leaned forward and kissed the top of Alfie's head.

"Okay. We can go now." Alfie jumped to his feet and offered me his hand. I twined my fingers around his and gingerly walked across the slippery trail.

"Dad! Dad." Alfie left my side, racing toward his dad, who stood precisely where I had left him. Relief flooded his face, and his eyes shone. He knelt in the snow, gathering Alfie into his arms.

Tinsel raced around the three of them, yipping playfully.

"Dad, who's that?" Dash pointed toward me.

"We met the other day. My name is Mary Christmas." I shook each boy's hand. "But you can call me Mary."

"Is that your real name?" Alfie's eyes widened.

"It is so. It's a Christmas name." I giggled.

"I'm Dash, and that's my brother. His name is Alfred." Dash nodded his tousled head.

"No, it's not. My name is Alfie." Alfie poked his brother's arm, knocking him into the snow.

"Those are elf names. I know that for a fact." I folded my arms across my chest and nodded.

The boys stared, their mouths hanging open.

Christopher locked eyes with me, and his gaze filled with gratitude, warmth, and, most of all, love. Everything I had ever longed for was within my grasp—all I needed to do was open my arms and welcome it. I turned and walked away.

* * *

Lincoln Frost stood on the top step of the gazebo in the town square, tapping his microphone and smiling. Chelsea and three town counselors beside him. People lingered in groups of twos and threes, and mothers shushed their children. I stood safely out of range beneath the pavilion while the merry-go-round sang.

"Welcome to Forest Falls on this wonderfully snowy day. I hope everyone enjoyed the pancake festival. I know I did." Lincoln chuckled. "Congratulations to the turkey winners and those leaving with one of these stunning floral arrangements. I want to celebrate a wonderful year in Forest Falls as the holidays begin. Welcome to our sixteen new residents, including my brother-in-law, Christopher. Where are you, Christopher? Say hello." He looked across the sea of heads as the crowd responded with clapping hands.

"Hey, Einstein." Big Tree stood head and shoulders above the crowd.

Lincoln cleared his throat. "On behalf of the town council, I'm excited to announce that we have approved funding to construct a brand-new community center encompassing a larger ice surface and indoor tennis and pickleball courts."

I looked sideways and smiled at Mrs Sandusky, who chattered with her husband.

"I want to thank our community groups and local businesses for making events like the Festival of Lights possible. Let's ensure we spread kindness and joy to everyone around us this season. Speaking for the Council, staff, and my family. I wish you a safe and happy Christmas and a fantastic New Year." He gazed among the crowd while Chelsea, standing beside her husband, looked on.

"Hey, girl, why so glum?" Aredhel knocked my elbow as the crowds disbursed. She carried herself with an other-worldly elegance, her flaxen hair tumbling over her shoulders, not a strand out of place. Her double-breasted wool coat hung loose in a deep shade of burgundy wine. I glanced at the open-toed stilettos in wide-eyed wonder.

"Can we go somewhere? Somewhere quiet." I looked into her alluring eyes, unaffected by her charms.

"Sure. What's up?" She smiled, looking oh so pleased with herself.

"Riverwalk. Let's go." I clasped her elbow, dragging her toward the cafe.

Tinsel followed.

"Hey, watch the heels, huh? These were expensive." She stepped over the icy ruts on the road.

I glanced at the fuschia pink open toes, detailed with lacy chiffon flowerets.

The aptly named cafe, set far enough away from the busy downtown, overlooked a bend in the Pretty River. I breathed in the intoxicating aroma of coffee, whipped cream, and freshly baked croissants.

"What were you thinking, Aredhel? How could you?" I guided her into a corner booth overlooking the street.

"How could I do what?" She shrugged off her wool coat and set her leather sack on the seat beside her.

I gazed at her, and then I remembered the photographs.

"We'll have two lattes, please." She waved to the server.

"You dug up the info on the Maguire estate so that Christopher could buy it." I could not hide my despair. I sat back, lost for words.

"Oh, that." She twirled her fingers through her silken locks and laughed.

"What do you mean? Oh, that." I swallowed hard.

"Look. I had no choice. Well, okay, maybe I did." She tapped on the picture window, grabbing the attention of a dark-haired man in a grey trench coat. She batted her eyelashes and waved.

"What?" I pressed my hands to my forehead.

"It was Christopher. Your Christopher." She smirked at me.

"Excuse me. You don't even know Christopher." I searched my mind and could not find the connection.

"That's not true. I saw him that day on the mountain. What the elf, how long does it take to make a latte?" She craned her neck, scanning the back counter for the server.

"What day on the mountain?" My thoughts scrambled.

"When we were little? Another step, and he would have discovered the entrance to the Elven kingdom." She tossed her pretty head and laughed. "You tossed acorns at him. Do you remember? It was the first time you used your magic. You saved the Elven folk."

She was right. Of course, she was right—Christmas Mountain hid more than one secret. A deep crevasse veiled in shadow led to a labyrinth of underground caverns, a palatial world of waterfalls, verdant forests, and ivory castles where the Elven folk had existed for millennia. I had been there once.

I stared at the pretty elf. I had been so enamored by the cute boy that I hadn't realized Aredhel was there on that fateful day.

"You turned him around, and he left. I thought little of it until Jared tasked me with researching the Maguire Estate. I was going to bury the whole thing, but he was so excited about Christopher Northbrook moving back to town. And then your name came up." She shrugged her pretty shoulders.

"My name?" I closed my eyes. I could see where this was going.

"He told me Christopher had a thing for you. JoJo confirmed it. I made an executive decision, babe." She nodded, her sparkling eyes seeking forgiveness.

"He? As in Jared?" I sucked my bottom lip into my mouth and closed my eyes. I told myself this could not be happening. "You put all of us at risk, Aredhel." My tone mixed disbelief with rage. I glanced over my shoulder, ensuring the server was out of earshot.

"Hey, the guy loves you. Anyone can see it. Written in the stars, babe. How else did he escape the gloom? There was a reason for that." Her violet eyes brimmed with happy bliss.

I released the breath I was holding. What Aredhel said made sense. Christmas Mountain was private land, well-marked, with no trespassing or hunting signs. The Elven folk evoked an ancient spirit to ensure the uninvited stayed away. The entity lived and breathed within the tree line—the gloom. Those who dared venture within would soon find themselves engulfed in a cloying mist with nowhere to run, nowhere to hide. The gloom invaded their thoughts, filling their minds with tortured visions. Their worst nightmares came true. I had heard the screams.

People talked. People learned to stay away.

And yet Christopher had crossed the boundary unscathed, following the tumbling stream toward the summit, to where he found me, or I saw him, steps away from discovering the true secret of Christmas Mountain.

"You know the Elves will never leave the place alone.

The Maguires built directly on a hallowed path." My grand-father had warned the newly married couple that they were building their dream home on sacred ground and that no good would come of it, and he was right—the Maguires had abandoned the house within the year, terrified of the nightly happenings. The Elven folk took their fairy paths seriously.

"I know. But now he has you." She shrugged her shoulders, giving no more thought to the Elven ways.

"Oh, Aredhel. What have you done?" I rested my nose on my clenched fists. There was no going back from this.

"Hey, he got it for a song. It's not a big deal." She flicked her hands in the air just as the server arrived with two steaming lattes adorned with swirling hearts.

Chapter Six

Christopher

I engaged the gas pedal, launching the Land Rover over each rise, which sent the kids into fits of six-year-old laughter. The Seven Sisters, the road in and out of Forest Falls, was like a roller coaster with steep dips and rising inclines. I coasted to a stop approaching the crossroads.

Above the tallest tree stood the water tower, a round white drum splashed with big black letters reading, "Welcome to Forest Falls."

I honked the horn, waving at the early arrivals. Big Tree coasted down the icy pond, pushing a shovel. Guilt washed over me. I should be there with the guys, helping to prepare the pond for today's event.

I tapped the steering wheel and pushed the guilt away. My desire to see her sooner rather than later propelled me toward Christmas's Christmas Tree Farm. I had tossed and turned all night, her name a whisper on my lips.

"Is that the pond, Dad? Is that where we're going? Can we play hockey, too?" Dash looked out the window.

"You bet we are, but first, we'll see Mary and find the perfect Christmas tree for our new house. You remember Mary and Tinsel." I glanced into the rearview mirror, looking for their reaction.

"I love Tinsel." Alfie smiled. "Can we get a dog, Dad?"

I engaged the wipers, clearing snow from the windows, her image flashing in my mind's eye. I followed the directional arrow pointing toward Christmas's Christmas Tree Farm.

"There is so. There is so." Alfie's voice rang out over the holiday tunes blasting from the radio.

"What's the matter? Why are you arguing?" I glanced over my shoulder.

"Dash said there's no such thing as Santa Claus." Alfie's voice rose.

"What? Why would you say that, Dash? Of course, there's a Santa Claus." I kept my gaze on the road, hiding a smile.

"No, there isn't, Dad. Auntie Chelsea said so." Dash shook his head.

"Well, Auntie Chelsea is wrong. The big man is real. I met him myself when I was your age." I thought of all my Christmas memories from childhood and how my parents carried on the tradition—Dad dressing up as Santa Claus, Mom preparing cookies for Santa, and carrots for the reindeer. For years, I believed.

"But Auntie Chelsea, she said—" Dash bounced in his seat.

"Auntie Chelsea doesn't believe in Santa. That's why she said that. But I do. If you believe in Santa, he will come.

Do you believe me?" I glanced backward and saw two innocent faces so filled with trust.

"I believe you, Dad." Alfie nodded.

"Dash?"

"Me too, Dad. I told Auntie Chelsea she was wrong." Dash shook his head.

I wheeled into the long laneway and ground to a stop, filled with a sudden rush of happiness. It was as I remembered: buttery yellow siding roofed with mossy green shingles draped in snow, a covered porch swagged with greenery and twinkling with lights, and two flower pots sprouting plastic candy canes—so very Mary.

"Are we in a fairy tale?" Alfie's eyes widened.

"Look—horses. Dad, can we get a horse?" Dash stared at the two Clydesdales, their broad white faces striking against their rich mahogany coats, harnessed to a straw-filled sleigh.

"A fairy tale?" I slowed the truck, gazing into the snow-covered valley, dense with greenery. White pines towered over the conical spruce, their gnarled branches holding up the sky. Christmas Mountain climbed into the clouds, the rugged terrain best suited to billy goats.

"Fairy tales have happy endings, Dad." Alfie referred to the stories his grade one teacher told, the same ones he reiterated every night before bed.

"They do not." Dash crossed his arms.

"Yes, they do. Miss Gagnon said so." Alfie spat, his voice laced with certainty.

"Look, guys. Look at the deer." I lowered the windows and pointed at the feathery branches buried in snow and the deer wintering in the hollows of the enormous trees.

Tinsel barked, running down the driveway to greet the car. I recognized Nick, the white-haired man with a long white beard, who had been a fixture at the farm for as long as I could remember. His resemblance to Santa Claus was uncanny. I recalled her question. "Do you believe in Santa Claus?"

"Here we are." I pulled into the designated parking spots, each adorned with a plastic candy cane. Before I unbuckled my seatbelt, the boys had already escaped from their seats.

"Hey, wait for me." I retrieved their hats and found their mitts strewn on the floor. "Stop," I called out, and to my surprise, they slid to a grinding halt. I handed Alfie the blue hat and Dash the orange. I tilted my head, giving them a look as they tugged on their mittens.

"Can we pat the horses, Dad? Can we?" Dash tugged my sleeve.

"No wandering off, okay? Is everyone on the same page?" I gazed at them. "There will be no repeat of yesterday."

"We know, Dad. Okay, Dad." Two serious faces nodded in agreement.

"It wasn't my fault, Dad." Alfie stood straighter and crossed his arms. "You said we could."

"I did not say you could go skating without me." I lifted my brows. "Don't tell lies, Alfie. Santa's elves are listening."

A howling gust pushed me toward the farmhouse.

"Good morning, Nick. I'm not sure you remember me. Christopher, Christopher Northbrook." I extended my hand as a gesture of goodwill.

Nick's grip was that of a young man.

"Of course, I remember. You were once a fixture in these parts. I understand you're moving back." He nodded at the distant Maguire place, the gabled roof visible on the next hill.

I gazed over the field, planted with Scotch Pine, and at

the house in the distance—our home, mine, and the boys. There was no going back. I moved in the last boxes yesterday.

"We're getting settled in. Well, as much as we can with the state of things." I rubbed my chin, considering my quick decision. Was it too rash?

"That's great news." He looked over the fields and back at me.

The silent pause grew.

"These are my boys, Alfie and Dash." I motioned between the two twins, who leaped from one snowbank to another.

"Well, hello, and Merry Christmas." Nick extended his hand toward Dash. "Will you young fellas be chopping down your own Christmas tree?" His blue eyes twinkled.

"Yes, sir." The two boys hollered, jumping up and down in the snow.

Tinsel yipped.

"Shush now." Nick quieted the dog.

She sat on her haunches, her eyes bright, her pink tongue lolling.

"Tinsel." Alfie dropped to his knees, wrapping his arms around her neck.

"Is Mary about, Nick?" I looked at the farmhouse, the mullioned windows wrapped with cheery lights, and the door adorned with a wreath of silver bells. A four-foot penguin, wearing an elf hat and wrapped in a winter scarf, stood beneath the covered roof, holding a welcome sign.

"You'll find her in the barn. How about I show these young ones the trappings of a real sleigh?" He winked at me, the twins following him toward the two Clydesdales. Tinsel yipped and nipped at their heels, corralling the two boys.

I waited momentarily, worried they might be too much for Nick to handle, but my concern soon faded. Nick pointed to the horses and led the boys around the sleigh. They climbed up and then hopped down. Under Nick's tutelage, they stroked the gentle giants, offering them apples. Their giggles floated toward me on a gust of breeze.

I walked across the yard, the red barn looming larger by the moment. After the disaster yesterday, how could I face her?

An orange cat leaped through the open barn door. With its hackles raised, the cat danced sideways and then jumped into the shadows.

I inhaled aromatic straw and earthy dust laced with the faint smell of ammonia. The wind whistled, drifting in from one end and out the other. Despite my insulated parka, I shivered.

I continued through the wind tunnel, searching for her.

I lost track of her yesterday, too stunned and taken aback even to think straight. After she had found Alfie, she disappeared, and when I looked up, Chelsea stared me down. My sister. I swept her into my arms and hugged her for no reason other than I could. She dragged me and the boys to the front stage for Lincoln's speech.

"Good morning, Christopher." She looked up from inside a box stall, her eyes flashing with that familiar spark.

Shielded in canvas coveralls, her golden hair tucked beneath a woolen toque, she was the epitome of breathtaking. Her cheeks glowed, and her lips were a pretty shade of berry pink. She raised a pitchfork and deftly tossed soiled straw into a wheelbarrow.

"I'm a day late." I shifted to the other foot and offered the brand-new shopping bag.

"Huh?" She leaned on her pitchfork.

"Northern Spy. The grocer said these are the best for baking." I stopped at Del's Grocer at first light and, after much discussion with the aging grocer, learned which apples she would want to bake a pie.

"Oh, thanks. You can put them over there." She motioned toward a bale of straw at the end of the aisle. "It's a little early for pond hockey, right?"

"We're here for a Christmas tree. For the new place." I set the bag on the straw bale, gazing through the barn's back door at the breathtaking view of the wintry valley.

"Oh, right? How's it going?" She studied me, her gaze thoughtful.

"Well, we have running water. The fireplaces should kick out enough heat." I scanned each box stall piled with straw. I shifted sideways, maneuvering between the doorway and the wheelbarrow, and joined her.

"How are Alfie and Dash? After yesterday?" She tilted her head, searching my eyes.

"We had a conversation about wandering off." I met her gaze. "I don't know how to thank you. If it wasn't for Tinsel and you, of course...I've never felt that kind of fear before." I shook my head, still reeling from the scare.

She nodded and returned to her work, lifting the pitchfork and tossing soiled straw into the wheelbarrow.

There were so many things I needed to say. After our kiss in the park, she lived in my mind. I lifted my hand.

"What are you doing?" She raised her chin, staring me down.

"There's a piece of straw stuck in your hair." I tugged the yellow stick free and displayed it in my palm.

"Oh." Her lips parted in a whisper.

Hunger burned in my heart. For what was. For what could be? I had nothing to lose. I had everything to lose.

"There's something I wanted to tell you, not that it changes anything." I leaned against the half-wall with my arms folded.

"Oh. What?" She sent me a side glance.

"It happened a long time ago." The conversation played in my mind.

"Okay." An awkward silence filled the space.

"Chelsea mentioned you were getting married, and I took her word for it." I gazed at her, uncertain of the response I sought.

"Oh? What does it matter?" She huffed and turned from me.

"You're protecting her?" I raised one eyebrow, surprised by her reaction.

"She's not a happy person. She's never been happy." Sadness flickered over her face and sympathy.

"She single-handedly changed the course of my life." It struck me that my narrative was unjust and served no purpose. I blamed my sister for a decision I had made a long time ago. A wave of shame flooded my heart.

"Is that why you're not getting along? Is that why you moved into that old house? You should probably go before all the Christmas trees are gone." She motioned with her eyes, directing me toward the exit.

I scratched my forehead. Sometimes, staying quiet was the smartest move a man could make.

"Look, Christopher. You got on that train, and you left. You don't get to blame your sister, and you don't get a replay." Her voice trailed off, and she looked away.

"I'm asking for one." I pushed off the wall and reached for the pitchfork, stilling her over-the-top work ethic.

"You should go." She rolled her eyes, but her gaze softened.

"Would you have dinner this evening with us? After the pond skate?" Electricity sparked, tingling currents that stopped my heart.

"You and your boys have a tree to decorate." She swept the tip of her tongue over her bottom lip.

"I make a mean mac and cheese." The hairs on my nape rose, and the blood in my veins heated. Her nearness affected me like no other.

"You can't just jump back into my life." A slow smile crossed her face.

"I think I already have." My nose itched, and I resisted the impulse to sneeze.

"Yeah, we need to talk about that." She drove the pitchfork into the straw.

"When I asked you to marry me, you didn't say no." Seeing her today only solidified my decision. I lost her once. I wouldn't make the same mistake twice.

"I didn't say yes." She fluttered her eyelashes, sending me a sly smile.

"You said you couldn't leave." Her mere presence slammed into me, and my knees buckled. I yearned to hold her in my arms.

"I couldn't leave," she said in a flat, matter-of-fact voice.

"If I had stayed, would you have said yes?" My nose tickled, and my eyes watered.

"Rehashing the past doesn't change it." She tossed another pile of straw into the wheelbarrow, dust motes wafting in the frosty air.

I pinched the bridge of my nose and held my breath.

"You live alone, miles from town. Why didn't you find someone? Tony the butcher? He always had a thing for you. There were others. Big Tree, for one." The hairs inside my nostrils shivered. I shifted sideways and sneezed with a vengeance.

"Are you done?" Amusement danced in her eyes.

"You're a beautiful woman, Mary. Please explain why you chose to be alone for all these years." I threw my hand over my face and sneezed again and then again, tears running down my face.

"Bless you. And how I live my life is none of your business." She scooped another pitchfork of straw and threw it into the wheelbarrow.

"The other night, you wanted me to come home with you." I squeezed my nose, holding back another sneeze. "You were going to show me something." I gasped.

"It was a simple question: whether you believed in Santa Claus. You said no." She turned on her heels but had nowhere to go.

I ducked my head and sneezed one final time. "I'm sorry. This is wild. You're not harboring any reindeer here, are you?"

"Reindeer? Like Santa's reindeer?" She canted her head, set the pitchfork across the wheelbarrow, and brushed past me. She continued down the aisle and didn't look back.

"Caribou, a certain northern species. It's the only thing I'm allergic to. I've never encountered it this far south." I followed her into the aisle.

The wind whistled, followed by a hollow moan and a loud bang. I walked to the back door and looked over the windswept valley, discerning nothing unusual.

"What was that?" I wondered out loud.

Tinsel raced down the long aisle with the boys in hot pursuit.

"Dad. Dad. Look what Mister Nick gave us." Alfie and Dash flew to an abrupt stop at Mary's feet.

"Hey, guys. What have you got there?" She crouched on her heels and extended her hand.

The twins handed over their treasure, two iron horseshoes, their eyes wide with awe.

"Ah, yes. These are the right ones." She inspected one and then the other.

"The right ones?" Alfie looked at her.

"Some horseshoes hold magic." She held the horseshoes against the light.

"What kind of magic?" Their eyes widened, large and full of light.

"Christmas magic. The kind that makes wishes come true." Her eyes shimmered, her smile lighting up the surrounding space. "You need to hurry before the sleigh leaves without you. You'll want to find the very best tree."

"Okay, come on, Dad. Come on, Dad. Let's go." Dash grabbed my coat sleeve, pulling me with all his might.

"All right." I gazed into her sparkling eyes, memorizing every detail, wishing this moment could last forever.

* * *

Wood smoke drifted in a cloudy sky, and the aroma of roasting hot dogs wafted through the air. I skated across the pond, my legs burning.

I looked up and into the crowd, picking out familiar faces from years ago. Young and old huddled around the frozen pond, cheering for their team. I leaned into one powerful gust of wind, my heart pounding.

I held my breath, anticipation mounting, as the two towns fought for the honor of winning the Giant Candy Cane. I missed the camaraderie of small-town living. It's something the boys had never encountered.

With three minutes left in the game, the referee, dressed in black and white stripes, dropped the puck at center ice. Sticks jostled, and Big Tree won the draw. He shot the puck past Beacon Hill's defenseman. It was a game of cat and mouse, with Beacon Hill jostling for puck ownership.

It was a play I remembered well.

My lungs burning, I went deep into the other team's end, out-skating the defenseman.

Sixty seconds left on the clock.

I retrieved the puck and skated around the opposing team's net, slipping the puck back to Beans, who made a shot pass in my direction.

The crowds roared, waving red and white candy canes in the air. I spotted Mary, Alfie, and Dash with Tinsel by their side.

The goalie dropped between the pipes with his legs spread in a butterfly position.

"Go, Forest Falls. Go, Forest Falls." The onlookers roared their encouragement.

I tasted the win. There for the taking.

Taking advantage of the shot's momentum, I slammed the puck, redirecting it over the goalie's shoulder and into the net, and scored the game-winning goal.

The horn sounded, and the crowd cheered.

Forest Falls held onto their title for another year.

Chapter Seven

Mary

Clouds, illuminated by a crystal moon, drifted across a velvet sky. The house, capped in a blanket of snow, sat silent, smoke spiraling from the double chimneys. A storied past and rumored hauntings ensured the farmhouse held onto its mysterious allure. Some said ghosts chased the Maguires out of town. I knew differently.

I gazed at the roofline, drawn by a persistent sound echoing through the night—a broken shutter flapping with each gust of wind against the clapboard siding.

Instead of walking up the path and ringing the doorbell, I stood, shrouded in the darkness, second-guessing my entire life.

I had stopped short of sharing the Christmas secret, saved by Christopher's high school buddies. I shook my head, realizing how close I came to blurting out the truth.

No rational adult would think Santa Claus existed. Christmas magic was for children—for as long as they believed. My heart clenched when I thought of those little boys, Alfie and Dash. In their presence, the magic shimmered and bubbled over.

And Aredhel? OMG. I told myself her intentions were good. I slammed the knocker twice.

"Well, hello, I didn't expect you. The boys are asleep." The door opened, revealing the man of the house, looking more than fine in a white T-shirt tucked haphazardly into dark, tapered jeans and wearing white lace-up running shoes. His face lit up, giving me the courage I so desperately sought.

"This is for you. Happy Housewarming." I hovered on the threshold, gazing beyond him into a foyer stacked with cardboard boxes. I thrust the basket toward him.

"Candles? Wine?" He lowered his chin, inhaling the fragrant scent of homemade bread made fresh this morning. "A broom?"

"To sweep away all of your troubles." I smiled, steeling my resolve. There was no going back.

"Are you coming in?" He turned, placing the basket on top of a cardboard box.

"Oh, I shouldn't. I have an early day." I followed him into the foyer and paused, breathing in the fresh scent of pine. My breath curled into the air, and I suppressed a shiver.

"I know you're not working tomorrow. Christmas Eve is your day off. Give me your coat." He extended his hand.

"Okay, for a minute." I shrugged my coat over my shoulders and kicked off my boots. My nipples tightened, and my skin tingled from the chill, or was it his intoxicating scent? I followed him into what was once a grand space, now marred with yellowed wallpaper and water-stained ceilings.

The center hall plan was like mine: a rambling kitchen

on one side and a living room on the other. A circular stair-case led to the bedrooms above.

I craned my neck, my gaze drawn to the presents under the tree—the four presents I had wrapped just the other day. So much has happened since then.

"This place has sat empty for years. What are you going to do with it?" I asked, even though I knew things would turn sour. Hauntings were one thing—the Elven folk were another. No one strolled over their land uninvited.

"I'm going to fix it. I had plans drawn up. Let me show you." He retrieved a hanger from the closet and hung up my coat, gazing at me with hunger in his eyes.

My lips were parched. I couldn't think straight.

"Fix it?" I put two words together into a coherent sentence. I turned, finding him standing a heartbeat away.

"I'm here to stay." He took my hand and led me around the room. "I'm going to beam this ceiling and remove this partition wall. The view will overlook the valley."

"I can't believe it's still livable." I looked from one decrepit wall to another.

"Oh, it's not really. The furnace needs replacing. But at least the plumbing works." He smiled back, excitement dancing in his voice.

"So, you're living here with no heat? You can't stay here, not with two little boys." I swept my fingers through my hair, doubt niggling in my mind. He deserved the truth before this project of his went too far.

"You sound like my sister." He jutted his chin, his stubborn streak shining through. "There's nothing wrong with three men roughing it—nothing at all."

"Okay. Okay. You know where to find me if you need a cup of sugar." I ran my fingertips over the mantel, inscribed with intricate swirls, warmed by the crackling fire. A bursting ember made me jump backward and into the hard wall of his chest.

"We used to dream of living here. Do you remember the plans we made?" He circled his arms around me, spooning me from behind, enveloping me in a warm, masculine scent of soft leather and woodsy spice.

"Christopher." I sank into him, stirred by a desire I could not deny.

"I need you, Mary." He groaned and caught my bottom lip, the rich stubble on his chin teasing my senses. His nose glided along my nape while his lips left a trail of hot kisses.

My eyes stung. I wanted him so badly. I turned into him, reaching beneath his T-shirt and gliding my hands over hard-packed, defined muscles.

"Do you know what you do to me?" His eyes darkened.

I captured his mouth and immediately regretted my enthusiasm. My teeth clacked against his, and my ears rang.

"Ow." My heart thudded so loud I wondered if he could hear it.

"Let me kiss you." He lifted my chin with his index finger, his muscles rippling under my fingertips.

Heat tore through me—so much heat.

He cradled the back of my head, drawing a line of kisses down my face. He moved rhythmically, his lips falling into a familiar dance. He explored thoroughly, brushing the inside of my mouth and tracing my tongue with his own.

This was another plane of existence, one where pleasure dwelled.

"Do you know what I see?" He brushed his lips across my forehead.

"Hmm?" The whimper rising in my throat demanded more—more of him. I trembled against him, my knees weak.

"A million beautiful nights." He cupped my breast, his

thumb circling the arrowed nub beneath the smooth silk of my blouse. "Will you be mine, Mary Christmas?"

"No" was never an answer. He turned me inside out.

"What's that?" I stepped back, the moment shattered by a splintering crack followed by a whooshing roar.

Glancing upward, his expression changed from confusion to concern. He broke away, following the gushing sound into the kitchen.

Water flooded onto the kitchen floor, spurting from below the kitchen sink. Drips fell from the ceiling.

"Oh, oh. We've got trouble." He lunged under the counter, searching for the shut-off, and returned with the broken valve in pieces.

"Where's the main?" I looked at the basement door.

"In the basement." He sprinted down the stairs, his feet pounding each tread.

I opened the cupboard doors, searching for pots, bowls, and anything else to catch the rain falling from the ceiling. I found one ragged tea towel.

He returned, his face stricken with horror, cobwebs stuck in his hair. "It seems the pipes have broken."

"Look, come and stay at my place. I have lots of room. The boys will love it, with the horses and Tinsel. They'll have a ball." I nodded my head, convincing him with my smile.

The ceiling cracked and then gave way, and plaster and insulation landed with a resounding splat on the tiled floor. I jumped back, pressing flat against the wall.

"I guess I could use that broom right about now." He scratched his forehead, and then a grin formed on his face.

"You can't sleep here." Laughter bubbled up inside me, contagious laughter. "I'm sorry. This is just too funny."

"I haven't forgotten what you said." He curled me in his

arms and, amid the puddling water, kissed me fully and completely, setting my heart on fire. Then he pulled away, leaving me gasping. "Was there something you wanted to show me?"

"Um, yes, and the timing couldn't be more perfect." I buried my face in his chest and breathed him in.

* * *

Wind whispered through the treetops while wooden chimes tinkled from the rafters of the covered porch. Yellow light beamed from every window, and a holiday playlist filled the night with Christmas cheer. For me, the festivities took a backseat. My secret—the one I had so valiantly kept for so long was about to bust open.

"Do you need help?" I folded my arms across my chest, my heart stuck in my throat. Part of me said to turn him around and send him on his way, while the other wanted to hold him in my arms forever.

"We're good." He looked up from his parked car and shot me a wide smile.

He retrieved Alfie and Dash from the backseat, an overnight bag slung over his elbow. Alfie rested his head on his father's chest, drowsy with sleep. Dash, his smile bright, jumped onto his father's back, his short legs wound around Christopher's waist.

I smiled, realizing that in his haste, he had forgotten their boots. Their little feet, tucked into footed pajamas, poked out from their orange snowsuits.

"Hi, guys. Merry Christmas." I stepped aside, giving the three of them room to untangle.

"I can't thank you enough, Mary. Boys, say hello." He

set them on the braided carpet and removed woolen toques from their heads, letting loose their dark curls.

Alfie shrugged out of his snowsuit while Dash stared wide-eyed across the living room and beyond the Christmas tree, sparkling with silver and twinkling with lights.

"Oh, I like your pajamas." I smiled at their reindeer onesies. "They look cozy."

"Are we having a sleepover?" Alfie yawned and rubbed his eyes.

"You bet we are. And guess what?" I searched the coat rack for an empty hook.

"There are guests here who can't wait to meet you."

"Are they sleeping over, too?" Dash glanced at me, his gaze drifting toward the four elves, clad in red tunics trimmed with green and adorned with snowflake buttons, sitting at the card table, playing a fast game of Snap.

"No, they can't stay. They're leaving soon." I touched their shoulders, pressing the two boys forward. "This is Alfie, Dash, and their father, Christopher."

Christopher stood beneath a sumptuous ball of mistletoe, staring in disbelief into the room overflowing with Santa's elves.

"Snap. I got you this time," Marley yelled when Kirby slapped a yellowed card with a reindeer image face up on the table.

"Holly Hannabell, Marley. That's three times." Willow reached for a candy cane, sucking noisily on the end.

Two others sat cross-legged, bent over a wooden checkerboard. They looked up with soft brown eyes, their pert lips curving into graceful bows.

Hollis turned away from the Christmas tree. She ran her hand through her shiny brown hair, revealing a reindeer earring hanging from her pointed ear.

Green garlands, resplendent with lacy cedar and feathery pine and glistening with ruby red berries, wreathed the paned windows. Roped around the bushy branches, a string of blue lights flickered, spreading a magical glow. Notes of cinnamon spice hung in the air.

Nick peered through his spectacles at an ancient leather-bound tome resting on the long wooden table, poring over a scroll of names. "Well, if it isn't Alfie and Dash. Come in. Come in. Let me introduce you to some of my helpers." He motioned with a sweeping welcome. Nick resembled a jolly old elf, resplendent in his red suit fringed with white lambswool.

"Santa?" Alfie whispered.

Nick winked.

"As long as I've known him." Hollis chimed in.

"Are you Santa Claus?" Dash asked, his eyes wide.

"Mary? Who are these...these people?" Christopher's face flushed, and his voice filled with awe.

"Let me do the introductions." Nick nodded. "This is Hollis and Marley." He gestured at the two elves playing checkers. "They take care of the reindeer. Over there, we have Kirby, Willow, and Wish, who are in charge of wrapping presents. And this young man is Jory. He bakes all the cookies." He motioned to the card table.

"Would you like to play a game?" Clad in a red dress cinched with a green bow, Hollis sprang to her feet. Her pointed shoes jingled with silver bells.

"Who looks after the sleigh?" Alfie looked at Nick, his tone inquisitive.

"Who builds the toys?" Dash lifted his chin, looking at each elf.

"Oh, that would be Pinecone, Snowball, and Juniper. And then there's Harper, Morgan, and Peyton. Peyton's in charge of the sleigh." Hollis smiled, her round eyes beaming, her cheeks rosy pink.

"Would you boys like to see something?" Nick flipped the vellum pages of the heavy book. "This is your name right here, Alfie. And there's yours, Dash."

"Are you really Santa?" Alfie gave him a piercing gaze.

"Of course he is. Look at his suit." Dash planted his hands on his hips.

Tinsel brushed past the Christmas tree, knocking the glass baubles. The branches swayed.

"Oh, oh." Marley dived, saving the silver ornament from crashing onto the floor.

"Is this what I think it is? Is Nick the man in the red suit?" Christopher squeezed my hand.

"He is the real deal." I nodded, unable to hide my grin.

"No, it can't be. It just can't." He rubbed his head, confusion drifting through his eyes.

"Tinsel, be good," I called out as she bumped against Alfie's hip, demanding his attention.

"Hi, Tinsel. I've missed you." Alfie wrapped his arms around her silver ruff.

"Where's my dad's name?" Dash peered into the pages.

"Look, your dad is right there, and here's your Auntie Chelsea." He pointed his index finger at the names written in swirling script.

"Auntie Chelsea doesn't believe in Santa." Alfie buried his face in Tinsel's fur.

"Oh, she used to, and that's all that matters," Nick said gently.

"How about a game of snakes and ladders?" Marley reset the board.

"How about a cookie?" Willow leapt up.

Christopher's gaze darted from one elf to another, landing on me. He swept his fingers through his hair.

"Can we, Dad?" Dash followed Willow to the overflowing platter.

"Sure, but just one, and then off to bed." He regained his voice.

"Would anyone like hot chocolate?" I glanced around the room, smiling inside.

Dash slid into a chair beside Marley, leaning his elbows on the table and kicking his feet back and forth. Alfie plopped onto the floor, patting Tinsel and whispering into her ear. Nick smiled at me and then returned to his scroll of names.

Christopher turned away, his face slack. He strode across the foyer toward the hall table, where a table lamp threw yellow light on a leathered guestbook.

"This book. It goes back generations. Look at these dates. 1869. 1894. 1901." He flipped the pages—entry after entry, advancing from ink quill to fountain pen to penned ink. "Look at this. Thank you for the wonderful stay. The cocoa was wonderful. Hollis Elf, Christmas 1908." He gazed across the room at Hollis, who offered Alfie a bowl of red and green gumdrops. "She can't be that old... can she?"

"Well." Where to begin?

"How long..." His voice drifted off.

"Help me with the hot chocolate." I pressed his elbow, guiding him into the kitchen.

"Your grandfather, his father before him." He laid his palms on the countertop. "I don't understand."

"I know." I rested my hand on his arm.

"I don't get it. This is...." He turned into me, dragging the back of his knuckle down my face. "The boys. What if they..." He said in a slow voice, his mind absorbing the unbelievable.

"They won't. They'll remember a dream, a wonderful dream." I lifted the pot from the stove, pouring warm cocoa into child-sized mugs. I found the candy sprinkles in the spice cabinet.

"Here." I handed him the can of whipped cream.

I backed him up, shaking red and green sprinkles over swirls of whipped cream.

"A dream.... yeah. It was just a dream." He clutched the steaming tray and followed me into the living room.

"Here we are." I took the tray from him and set it on the sideboard next to a platter of gingerbread men. "Hollis, can you watch the boys for a few minutes?"

"They're fine with us." Her smile lit up the room.

"There's something I want to show you," I whispered into Christopher's ear.

"There's more?" His gaze drifted back to me.

"Put this on." I handed him his coat and slid into mine, closing the door firmly behind us and leaving the warmth behind.

"Is this the secret? That thing you wanted to show me?" He pressed his arms tight against his sides.

"This is the secret." I glanced sideways, unable to keep a straight face, grinning like a kid on Christmas morning.

The snow crunched underfoot, and a gentle wind blew kisses across the barnyard. The trees, bathed in moonlight, stood in silence.

"Where are we going?" He looked into the sky, twinkling with a million stars.

"Well, I hope you have a tissue in your pocket." I pressed my hands against the rough wood, sliding the barn door open. The track grumbled in protest.

He didn't fully understand. But he would soon enough.

I flicked the lights, illuminating the long aisle in incandescent light. Molly ignored our presence—Big tossed his mane, welcoming us with a loud whinny.

"How are you, big guy?" I rubbed the soft spot behind Big's ear.

"What are we doing here?" He stamped his feet and shivered.

"Look down there." I motioned to the box stalls at the other end of the barn.

I followed leisurely, my lips pinned together, hiding my smile.

"No. It can't be." He gripped the iron bars, his voice barely audible.

Heavy antlers covered in velvet crowned the reindeer's majestic head. The reindeer studied him through soft chocolate eyes—eight more slept peacefully, nestled in a thick bed of straw.

"It's exactly what you think." I touched his fingers—a pang of longing tore through me.

"Reindeer? Eight reindeer. And the sleigh?" He smiled —his expression a mixture of confusion and wonderment.

"Nine. Come with me." I dragged him through the back door.

My gaze lifted toward the crystal orb and Christmas Mountain—a white fang clawing the night sky.

"What is it?" Christopher bent his head into the wild gusts.

"Help me with this." I pushed the heavy door.

He offered his strength, and the heavy slab slid open.

"Here it is." Santa's sleigh sat ready for flight, its red paint glistening in the moonlight, silver runners glimmering.

"This can't be." His breath caught, his expression

shifting from disbelief to understanding. He ran his fingers over the swirling edges and the soft leather lining the bench seat. He bent at the waist and whistled, admiring the shining undercarriage.

"It's the real deal." I smiled, his amazement filling my heart.

He walked toward me, his eyes reflecting the moon's light.

The branches rustled overhead as a flock of black-capped chickadees took to the skies.

It was time.

I breathed in the magic, the cold of winter, and the tang of the night. Raising my arms, I called the storm. The wind screamed in answer.

The mist played its part, rising from the underworld, wispy fingers reaching over the land, finding its place between heaven and earth, icy crystals feathering a star-studded sky in a gossamer veil. Basked in shadow, the snow-crusted valley shimmered beneath an eerie moon.

His grip on my arm tightened.

A team of reindeer raced soared above the treetops, carrying Old Nick and his elves on their homeward journey north—even the wind stopped to listen.

The wind gentled. Snowflakes waltzed to the ground in playful, frothy clusters.

"Mary?" His face blanched. His eyes filled with shock.

"This is why I can't leave." I grabbed his hand, following the glimmering path.

"It's real. All of it. The reindeer. The elves." He dragged the door open, revealing an empty drive shed.

"Yes." I walked ahead and into the barn. Molly and Big stamped their feet.

"The reindeer. Where did the reindeer go? How did this happen?" He stared into the empty stalls.

"Are you okay?" I stood beside him, understanding his confusion. I half expected him to walk out the door and never return.

"You. How did you do it?" He dropped onto a straw bale.

"I don't know. I can't explain it. The magic runs with the Christmas name. I'm the only one left. Let's check on the boys, yeah?" I walked away, leaving him to ponder my situation. It was a question I couldn't fully answer. I needed him to understand.

He caught up with me on the back porch.

"Mary." He placed his hand on my lower back, turning into me, facing me. His eyes darkened, and his lush lips parted.

I shivered at the contact, tingling from his nearness and the magic still radiating from my fingertips. "Look." I motioned down the long driveway.

A magnificent twelve-point stag stood in the moonlight, well-muscled and heavily furred. A golden light enveloped him, and then he was... gone.

"What was that?" He gripped my arm, pulling me against him, protecting me from harm.

"There are things you need to know about Christmas Mountain." I buried my face in his chest, a smile curving my lips.

The house was quiet and empty of visitors. The checkerboard sat on the coffee table, the checkers in play. The sound system sent holiday music in soft, melodic tones.

I took his hand and climbed the stairs to the second floor. Tinsel slept peacefully on the floor between two single beds in the first bedroom on the left, where Alfie and Dash nestled beneath red plaid comforters.

"How? Who?" He looked at both boys, the two water glasses on the night table, and the glowing nightlight.

"My money's on Hollis." I grinned. "Come on."

He followed me downstairs, stopping in the foyer.

"What is it?" I turned to him, aching for him.

"Look up." He nodded toward the mistletoe hanging in the archway, the voluptuous ball of leathery leaves, and the waxy white berries Jory had retrieved from a sacred oak deep within the forest on the first day of Yule.

I had a hunch which one, although Jory would not confirm it.

I wanted to throw myself into his arms and have my way with him. Still, I was hesitant, even after everything... I needed to know.

"Wait." I clasped his hands. "Are you okay with all of this?"

"That thing you had to show me?" He brushed his lips against my face, breathing me in and setting my world on fire. "This is it?"

"Yes, all of it.." I dropped my hands to my sides, fisting my palms—stilling the rampant need flowing through me.

"There is one way to ensure my silence." He cradled my head in his hands and caught my lips.

"And what's that?" I murmured into his hot breath, shaking almost violently, needing him more than anything.

"Marry me." He dipped his head, meeting my hunger with his own.

My thoughts unscrambled as the heat unfurled between us.

Chapter Eight

Christopher

Like a phoenix rising from the ashes, I awoke a new man. The future blinded me with its radiance—Alfie and Dash, Mary and I, and the children we would make together. With Mary nestled beside me, I stared into a star-studded sky at the shifting colors of night, pondering our existence in this world and the magic of another. Santa Claus, elves, and flying reindeer—she held a magical world at her fingertips.

I rolled onto my side, drinking in her beautiful curves, the ones I cherished over and over the night before. She owned my heart.

"You remembered the words." I leaned on my elbow, watching her in the dim morning light.

"The words?" She combed her fingers through her hair, the burnished mane cascading over one shoulder.

"The nickname. Sugarplum. Lollipop." I murmured. My cock throbbed for her, a line of fire thick against my belly.

"How could I forget?" She moved with silent grace, searching through a dresser drawer.

"Come back to bed." I tried to imagine my life without her and couldn't. My mouth watered for more of her taste. She robbed me of all rational thought. "You can't leave me like this." I shoved the cotton sheet aside.

"You're incorrigible." She pounced on the bed, resting on her knees and caging my hard erection between her muscular thighs.

"Do you know how much I love you?" I slid my hands over her smooth skin, cupping rounded globes. "What say you, Mary Christmas?"

"What say you what, Mr. Northbrook?" She flexed her hips, grazing my rigid length with her heat.

I hissed in response.

She dipped her head, her silken locks falling over her brow.

"Do you have any idea what you do to me?" I groaned as my balls burned.

"Hmm." She whimpered, licking the inside of my mouth

I drew her on top, repositioning her sweet sex over my mouth.

"What are you doing?" She clung to the headboard, rasping a quick breath.

"Making you come." I parted her inner lips, running my tongue up and down her folds.

"More. Oh, yeah." She moved rhythmically, her eyes heavy-lidded as she watched me pleasure her.

In the golden morning light, she was more than beautiful. My tongue traveled up to flick her clit, coaxing that sweet bud to swell.

"Yes, oh yes." Her inner thighs trembled as she shattered, her sweet heat flooding my lips, coating my tongue, and sliding down my throat.

She was exquisite.

"Come to me. Kiss me." I rose with her, sinking back against the headboard and brushing my lips against her face. "Last night was amazing."

She reached for my cock, fisting the width in her warm hand. She pumped the hard length until I thought I would explode.

"Do you know what you do to me?" I seized her waist, guiding her as she lowered her sex inch by inch onto my throbbing shaft, stretching her tight channel to accommodate my width.

"I know what you do to me." She moaned as her inner walls tightened, clutching and squeezing my cock.

She planted her hands over mine, plumping her swollen breasts, rocking greedily, her whimpers taking me over the edge.

"So, good." My breath caught in my throat when she rolled her hips, taking me deeper, inch by delectable inch.

With my cock buried deep inside, I lifted her from the bed. Reason left me when she wrapped her legs around my hips and clung to me.

Beads of sweat poured down my spine. It had been so long since I'd made love to a woman. But this was not any woman. This was the woman I loved.

I rested her bottom on the window seat. The rising sun trickled through the frosted panes, setting fire to her golden strands.

"More. More." She gripped two handfuls of my hair, dragging her lips over mine.

Her heated gaze raked my soul. She consumed me.

"Are you sure?" My breath shuddered, my face buried in her tumbling locks.

"I'm sure." She dragged her fingers down my back, her sex rippling, cusping on release.

I pulled out slightly and then thrust hard and deep, over and over again, stroking her harder and faster.

Only she could ease the ache.

Shivers danced over her skin, and her pussy shuddered, flooding my cock with liquid heat.

Delight shot through me, hot jets racked with agonizing bliss. My thrusts slowed, and I collapsed into her arms, heaving for my next breath.

Cool air kissed her flesh. She tormented me with every movement, exploring my nape and pressing slow kisses. She was my undoing.

"Marry me?" I thumbed her nipple. A simple yes would do.

"Christopher." She looked like a goddess, her eyes half-mast, her lips swollen pink. We exchanged a silent moment.

"Marry me." I walked my fingers through her lustrous waves, massaging the nape of her neck and upper shoulders.

"I can't leave." She leaned into my wandering touch, her voice rasping.

"Neither can I." I smoothed my palms over alabaster skin—delighting in a lazy, sensual ride.

"The secret?" she murmured, her voice low.

"Will be ours to keep." I licked the seam of her mouth, my shaft thickening, lengthening, my pulse hammering.

"The magic runs in my blood—in our children if we have them." Her intense gaze burned my soul.

"Marry me," I asked for the third time. I rested my hands on the curl of her hips, holding on for the rest of my life.

"Okay. Okay. I'll marry you." She peppered my face with kisses. "I love you, Christopher. I've always loved you."

A comet streaked through the sky. Or was that Santa's sleigh?

A deep woof and chortling laughter came from below in another part of the house.

"The boys are up. I can hear Tinsel." She sent me an amused glance. "It's Christmas Eve, you know."

"Yeah?"

"Santa Claus is coming. We have to get ready." She laughed, her eyes dancing.

The words she spoke were not lost on me. No longer singular. No longer alone.

Footsteps clattered. Paws thumped.

Bounding off the bed to the open dresser drawer, she retrieved her pajamas, sliding her arms and legs into them with the speed of a gazelle. Her face turned a delightful shade of pink.

I threw my legs onto the floor and slid into my sweats. Resting my hands on my knees, I readied myself for two active little boys.

"Dad, Dad, guess what? Hi Mary. We saw Santa's sleigh. We did, we did." Alfie and Dash jumped up and down.

"Well, it's Christmas Eve. Santa has a busy night ahead." I grinned at her.

"He could be halfway around the world by now." Alfie planted his hands on his hips, informing his brother.

Dash raced to the window, looking into the twilight sky.

"Who wants to help me feed the horses?" She turned to the boys.

"I do. I do." Alfie and Dash answered at the same time.

Tinsel barked.

"While you do that, I'll start breakfast. What will it be? Pancakes? French toast?"

"Do we have to go home, Dad? Can we stay with Mary?" Alfie sat on the braided rug and hugged Tinsel.

"Well, that's up to Mary, I think. Let's ask her."

"You can stay here for however long you want." She looked over her shoulder and smiled.

"With Tinsel?" Alfie shrieked.

Tinsel barked.

"What about Santa? How is he going to find us?" Alfie's gaze darted toward her.

"I think Santa can find you wherever you go and wherever you are, as long as you believe." My heart filled with happiness. Whatever came, we would face together—the Christmas secret safe in our hands.

"See, I told you so." Dash raced ahead and down the stairs, with Mary following.

I made the bed, pulling the duvet over the sheets and setting the pillows.

"Christopher?" She stuck her head around the door and into the room.

"Is everything okay?" I moved toward her.

"I called Chelsea and invited her and Lincoln for dinner. I hope you don't mind." She met me halfway, circling her arms around my waist.

"You did?" My heart warmed.

"I did." Her eyes smiled.

"You and I have an announcement to make." I skimmed her forehead with a light kiss.

"We do." She grinned. "It's time we spread some Christmas magic of our own."

"Every day." I breathed her in, my heart's content. "I love you, Mary Christmas."

"I love you too. I didn't know how to tell you." She buried her face against my chest.

"Dad. Dad. Come quick." Alfie called from the bottom of the stairs.

"Are you ready?" I folded my arms around her, pressing my lips to the crown of her head.

"More than ready." She lifted her chin and met my lips.

The perfect Christmas kiss.

About the Author

"I began my writing career in the pre-dawn of a winter morning while my husband snored like a train. We could call my husband the catalyst. If it weren't for him, I would never have gone to the kitchen to make a pot of coffee, feed the cat, and sit on the loveseat in front of the fire. It was there, in those moments of wondrous quiet, that I did something I had never thought possible. I opened my laptop, and while the coffee went cold, I wrote a story. My husband had no idea that these sojourns to the loveseat in front of the fire would become a daily occurrence, that writing would become an obsession, but the cat knew. She knows everything.

I write stories that make you laugh, make you cry, and make you love. Thank you, friends, for reading!

In the beginning, there was an empty page.

I am a writer who lives in Muskoka, Canada, with a husband who snores, a hungry cat, and an almost perfect canine. He's an adorable little shit.

Visit Hanna Park at
   www.hannapark.ca

Also by Hanna Park

Novels

Finding Tiegan

Novellas

Sorrento Seduction

Unwrapped in Roros

Acknowledgments

My heartfelt gratitude goes to my family, who support my writing obsession with humor and grace, and to my editor, Judi Mobley, who whips my words into shape.

Hanna's Awards
    2024 Heart's Award - Finalist
    2024 Passionate Plume - Finalist
    2023 American Fiction Awards - Winner
    2023 Passionate Plume - Finalist
    2022 Stiletto Contest - Winner
    2022 Paranormal Romance Writers Guild
    2021 NN Light Book Award -Winner